Diamond in the Dirt 3

By Cade'l

Published by Stone Ink
Printed in the United States of America

Carde'ls contact info:
Email: cardelunlimited@gmail.com
Instagram: @Card_e_l
Facebook: CardelWrites and StoneInkPublication

CHAPTER 1

On the day of Nyla McCoy's funeral the rain poured down out of the cloudy dark clouds in the sky. It was as if God was brokenhearted and cried his eyes out about the tragic end of one of his children. Nyla died at the age of 38 from a heroin overdose. Her family and friends were extremely shocked, they were all under the impression that she had been clean since the day she was released from rehab four and a half years ago. You know the famous saying: *What's done in the dark will come to light*. It's just sad that it took her to lose her life to reveal her deep dark secret.

Nyla wore an all white dress, and was laid out in a silver plated casket. She looked peaceful, just like she was sleeping. The pastor was standing in the pulpit preaching about an interesting philosophy pertaining to life and death and the power of God. The funeral was packed with family and friends that came from all over. Tadasia, Aunt Tasha, Uncle Bill, and Dynasty sat in the front pew reserved for the family only. Dynasty held her newborn daughter Zanyah gently in her arms.

Tadasia cried uncontrollably as she looked at her mother lay in the casket a few feet away from her.
"I can't believe this is happening," Tadasia cried, trying to wipe the tears from her eyes.

Tadasia tried her best to be strong and control her emotions but couldn't. It was as if the tears were forcing their way out of her puffy eyes. Tadasia was pretty much used to her mother being absent the majority of her life, but knowing that this would be her last time seeing her again stung her heart deeply.

Dynasty continued to rock her baby girl feeling a deep grief for the woman she loved like a mother. In fact she was probably a little more devastated than Tadasia. Dynasty was the one who discovered Nyla's unconscious body on the bathroom floor with the needle still stuck her arm.

Uncle Bill sat on the opposite side of his great niece. "Everything is going to be alright baby girl. You just have to be strong," he stated.

Uncle Bill was trying his best to comfort Tadasia. He and his sister Tasha immediately drove from down south to Trenton as soon as they got wind of the tragic news.

Dose, Snake Eyes, and Low Down sat close beside each other, a few rows behind the family's pew.
"I know my nigga sick to his stomach about his mom dying," Dose stated sadly looking at the pastor preach.

"Yeah I know, shit crazy," Snake Eyes sighed deeply as he slowly shook his head.

Snake Eyes suddenly noticed how everyone's attention was drawn towards the back of the church. It was Real walking in shackled at the feet and dressed in a bright orange jumpsuit that was drenched from all the rain. He was escorted up the aisle by three correctional officers assigned from the Mercer County Jail. Two of the officers walked close behind Real, while the other officer led in the front. The unforgettable sounds of the chains connected to the shackles rattled with every step he took. As Real walked up the aisle, he surveyed the crowd of people sitting in the pews and spotted Snake Eyes, Dose, and Low Down.

"What's good with my bail?" He asked.

"The bail is posted. The bail bondsman said you'll be out in 3 days," Snake Eyes responded loud enough for Real to hear him.

Real was so devastated by his mother's death, hearing that his million dollar bail was paid didn't even uplift his spirits.

The three correctional officers stopped in their tracks and stood a few feet away, allowing Real to pay his respects to his mother one last time. Real slowly stepped up to Nyla's casket and stood over top of her for a while. He sighed deeply as he stared down in to his mother's beautiful brown face.

"I'm so sorry mom," Real uttered sadly in a low tone as tears of guilt began to burn his eyes.

It was bad enough that Real's mother died from an overdose, but when the Trenton Times Newspaper mentioned that it was from a heroin package called *Super High*, it felt like his soul was snatched away and his heart was rotting inside his chest. *Super High* was his brand, so Real felt like he played a major roll in his mother's death. The only thing that kept him from taking his own life was the thought of his newborn daughter growing up without a dad.

Everyone at the funeral was focused on Real as he stood over his mother's casket. His eyes were closed and his head was tilted down while he silently prayed to God. Real wasn't praying for himself, he figured from all of the dirt he did in the streets he would be the last person on the planet God would send a blessing to. Instead, he made a desperate plea for God to forgive his mother for all her sins and allow for her to enter in to the pearly gates of heaven.

Real finally opened his teary eyes and turned to look at his family. Uncle Bill, Aunt Tasha, and Tadasia scooted down a seat so he could sit next to Dynasty and his daughter. Tadasia stood up and gave Real a tight hug.

"What's up baby," Real stated dryly before him and Dynasty gave each other a kiss on the lips.

Real looked into his daughter's beautiful face and his cold heart melted instantly. Not only did she look just like him, but this was his first time seeing her. Real had strictly forbid Dynasty from bringing his precious baby girl to the filthy ass county jail.

"You see daddy Zah Zah," Dynasty said in a sweet tone looking down in to her daughter's green eyes.

A wide smile brightened Real's depressed face as he lowered his head to kiss her on the forehead.

"Snake Eyes just said everything situated and I'll be out in three days."
"We know," Dynasty replied as she looked in to her man's sad eyes.

Dynasty had a whole lot to tell Real, but she knew that now was not the right time nor place.

After the funeral Real was escorted back to the county jail. It was in the early hours of the morning two days after Nyla's funeral, when Dose and three of Real's most loyal henchmen were murdered simultaneously in different locations.

CHAPTER 2

Tadasia picked Real up after he was released from jail and dropped him off at his house where Dynasty and his daughter were waiting. As soon as Real walked inside his house the first thing he did was soak his body in a hot bath. After this short period of relaxation, he ate the delicious full course meal Dynasty prepared for him.

Real was sitting on his black leather sofa holding precious Zanyah in his arms. He and Dynasty were watching a movie on their 60 inch flat screen tv. The overwhelming feeling of finally being able to hold his baby girl was unexplainable. He closed his eyes and breathed deeply out of his nose, making a silent vow to himself that he would never let anyone take him away from his family again. No matter what! He told himself he would rather die.

Real's heart was at peace thanks to the affectionate feeling of family love, but his mind was racing a million miles per minute. He kept asking himself over and over how did the police get enough evidence to charge him with the double murder. Real constantly replayed that fateful day back in his mind. A few people saw his face when he caught the two murders during the takeover after Kaze's death, but he knew the gun was never found because he gave it to Snake Eyes to get rid of it. He also wondered who in the hell killed Dose and his three henchmen.

Real wanted to call Snake Eyes and find out what was going on, but he told himself he was going to fall back for the day to gather his thoughts and spend some time with his family. He noticed Dynasty looking at him. "What's up baby, you alright?"

Dynasty was debating whether or not to tell Real that Snake Eyes tried to push up on her when he came to their house to drop Real's bail money off. *Fuck it, I'm just going to tell him,* she said to herself.

"Babe. When..."

Before Dynasty could finish, Real's attention was drawn to his cell phone that was vibrating on the table.

"Baby grab my phone for me."

Zanyah was sleeping peacefully in Real's arms and he did not want to disturb her. Dynasty quickly got up from the sofa to grab the phone and handed it to Real.

"Hello."

"A yo my nigga, I need to talk to you ASAP. It's real important," Snake Eyes said on the other end of the phone.

Real recognized who it was immediately.

"I already know what happened bruh. I'm in the crib spending time with the family. We'll link up and put everything together in a few days."

"I already know you know about Dose and them. I ain't talking about that. Some more bullshit just happened. Meet me down the street from your house in 10 minutes," Snake Eyes said sounding stressed.

Real sighed out loud frustrated. *If it ain't one thing, it's another,* he said to himself.

"Alright man, I'm heading out the door now."

Real hung up the phone and prepared to meet Snake Eyes. He handed the baby to Dynasty.

"Where the hell you think you going? And who was that on the phone?"

"I ain't going no where but down the street to meet up with Snake Eyes. I'll be right back."

It was pitch black dark outside and the wind blew lightly as Real walked down the quiet street. When he made it to the middle of the block he spotted Snake Eyes a few houses down with both of his hands behind his back. *There he go right there,* he said to himself. He also noticed a brown skin man with a bald head and no facial hair walking towards the porch steps of a red house. Real walked up to Snake Eyes.

"What's good bruh," Snake Eyes greeted.

"Shit, you let me know," Real responded.

Real began to step closer. Snake Eyes let out a loud wicked laugh and pulled out a chrome 12 gage shotgun from behind his back, pointing it at Real. BOOM! The 12 gauge slug crashed through Real's chest causing him to fly a few feet back.

"Agggh!" he groaned in agony.

Real's body came crashing down to the ground. Thick globs of blood poured from his mouth as he desperately gasped for air. Snake Eyes walked up on Real and stood over top of him with the shotgun pointed at his face. Real looked up in to the eyes of a real live snake and knew by his crazed look that his life was over.

"You ain't see this coming did you? You bitch ass nigga! Before I blow your fucking brains out your head, there's a few things I think you should know. I'm the one that killed Kaze bitch ass and served your dope fiend ass mom those bags of raw dope that killed her."

Snake Eyes began to chuckle as he taunted Real.

"All Benji had to do was just give me the connect and we wouldn't be going through all this."

Snake Eyes never got over his envy. He felt like he deserved the position that was given to Real.

"Now it's your turn to die nigga!"

BLOW! The gunshot had a different sound this time. It was from Wild Sal, who let off a shot from across the street with his chrome P90 Ruger. The slug hit Snake Eyes right in the face causing him to drop his shotgun and stagger. He placed his hand over the bullet wound in order to plug the hole and stop the bleeding.

Wild Sal had been following Real since he was released from jail, and was the man walking across the street towards the porch. The long dirty looking dreads and thick beard Wild Sal wore was a disguise all along. The clean look was his true identity, and unknown to all.

Suddenly, the loud sound of tires screeching came from a black Accord that came speeding out of the alleyway. The headlights were off when the driver slammed on the brakes, stopping in the middle of the street. Low Down waved his black .40 caliber handgun out of the window, aiming it at Wild Sal. He started letting loose. BLOW! BLOW! BLOW! BLOW! BLOW! BLOW! BLOW! Wild Sal swiftly ducked for cover behind a parked car. Snake Eyes managed to make it to the car and climbed inside. Low Down immediately slammed his foot on the gas and sped off recklessly down the street.

Wild Sal ran across the street to where Real was stretched out on the ground. He looked down to see all the blood pouring from Real's mouth.

"Fuck!"

This was the first time Sal had ever failed to protect an assignment. Real looked up at Sal and tried to speak, but the intense pain in his mid-section kept snatching his words away. He managed to snatch open the buttons on is hoodie, revealing the bullet proof vest he wore underneath. The pellets from the shotgun never entered Real's flesh, but the impact from the blast broke three of his ribs. A major sense of relief came over Wild Sal.

"Oh shit nephew, I thought it was over."

Wild Sal scooped Real from off the ground and took him back home. Once they got closer to the house Real saw that Dynasty was standing on the porch crying hysterically. After hearing the loud sounds of gun shots, she ran out to see if her man was okay. Seeing Sal carrying Real in his arms caused her to lose it.

"Calm down, he alright!" Sal shouted loud enough so she could hear.

Sal rushed up the steps and in to the house, placing Real on the living room couch next to his daughter. The commotion woke up the precious baby, and she began crying hysterically. Dynasty was still in panic mode.

"What happened?!"
"He was shot but the vest stopped the slugs from going through."

Sal tried to remain as calm as he could. He began taking off Real's hoodie and vest. Dynasty was rocking the baby, trying to quiet her crying.

"Sssh, mommy and daddy right here Zah Zah. We ain't going no where."

Dynasty already knew who was behind the hit, and regretted that she never got the chance to tell her baby dad how his so called friend and underboss tried to come on to her. Once the vest was removed, Sal saw how Real's left side was abnormally swollen.

"His ribs are broken."

Sal darted into the kitchen to get a bag of ice. Once he got back into the living room, he placed the bag of ice on the swollen area. When Real felt the cold ice a groan escaped his lips.

"Ahhhh!"

All he could do was lay his head back and stare up at the ceiling. Real's head hurt like hell, but he couldn't stop thinking about the chain of events that happened up to this point. He didn't want to believe it, but deep in his burning heart he knew he had no choice but to accept the truth. Real couldn't understand how or why he didn't see that Snake Eyes was a snake. All of these thoughts caused a burning and vengeful hatred to formulate in Real's bloodstream. *But what did he mean by 'all Benji had to do was give up the connect',* he thought confused, trying to make sense of everything.

CHAPTER 3

The full moon gleamed in the pitch black sky. The wind caused the leaves on the trees in Caldwalder Park to tremble. Real and Wild Sal sat close beside each other on the wooden bench near the swings and sliding board. "Damn man, what the fuck taking All Things so long," Sal exclaimed while looking at his watch.

The time was 12:40 A.M. which meant All Things was 10 minutes late. Wild Sal and All Things spoke a few days ago and planned to meet at the park to discuss what was going on. The situation was an unusual one, All Things never met up in spots like this especially at this time of night. Sal kept his eyes on the black entrance gate in hopes that All Things would walk through at any moment.

Real wore a black snorkel and was sitting patiently with his hands tucked inside his pockets staring up at the night sky. Wild Sal's frustration began to subside when he started thinking of all the drama Real was going through. *Damn this shit got nephew all fucked up in the head. I'm just going to wait to tell him, he got too much on his plate right now,* Sal thought to himself. When Real recapped that devastating night, he explained to Wild Sal how Snake Eyes gained his trust just to put the ultimate double cross down on him. Sal always felt that something wasn't right about Snake Eyes and it turned out he was right. He couldn't imagine how sick Real was feeling inside.

Real couldn't get his mind off of his enemy. *Why the fuck is all this bullshit happening to me*, he asked himself feeling broken in spirit. The venom from Snake Eyes' poisonous bite was slowly eating him alive from the inside out. When Real went to gather his money and drugs from his stash houses, he found that Snake Eyes had beat him to it. Real was desperately broke. He didn't even have enough money to fill up his gas tank. With all of the men in Real's elite circle knocked off, Snake Eyes was able to position the young hustlers and gangsters from his crew on the profitable blocks to supply the area with coke and dope. Even though Real was able to figure out his enemy's strategy, there were still certain questions that went unanswered. Like why didn't Snake Eyes just leave him in jail to rot. One thing's for sure, he told himself that he would make Snake Eye's regret and pay for his miscalculated decision with his life.

Suddenly, bright headlights began flickering from across the field.

"What the fuck," Wild Sal said.

He gripped the black Uzi that was concealed under his army fatigue jacket. Real gripped the chrome twin .40 caliber handguns that were in his coat pockets. Both men peered at the black Caprice parked near the basketball court.

"That must be him. Come on," Real said.

The two men stood up from the bench and began walking towards the parked vehicle.

All Things sat in the backseat wearing an all black suit with black leather gloves. A grin slowly came across his face after he saw how Real and Wild Sal hesitated before they finally walked towards the car. With all that was going on, All Things thought it would be wise to arrive in the park an hour earlier than the scheduled time. There were certain things that caused All Things to be suspicious about the meeting so he made sure to have snipers on guard.

"You see them Marlene," he asked the female driver.
"Yeah I see them," Marlene responded in a strong Spanish accent.

Marlene The Monster was the first lady and silent assassin of the notorious drug organization All Things ran in the state of Delaware. Real and Wild Sal never knew she existed, it was very seldom that people outside her circle saw her. Her name alone caused people to imagine a beastly and manly looking female, but her physical appearance was the total opposite. She was 5 foot 7, with a curvaceous petite frame, flawless bronze skin, long jet black hair that hung down to the middle of her back, and a beautiful face. She was also very soft spoken, and always had an ice cold look in her eyes.

All Things rolled down the dark tinted window and stuck his shiny balled head out the window.
"It's me, hurry up and get in."

Real climbed in on one side while Wild Sal got in on the other, putting All Things in the middle. Sal and Real noticed the female in the driver's seat and tried to get a glimpse of her face, but the black ski mask she wore prevented that. They both had a puzzled look on their faces knowing that All Things never brought anyone with him when they met up to discuss business. *Well shit, whoever she is she must be official*, Real thought to himself knowing All Things was always on top of his game.

"So what's going?" All Things asked.

Real sighed deeply and put his head down for a few seconds.
"It's a long story, but I'm going to try to keep it short and give you the basics," Real said.

All Things could tell by looking in Real's eyes that whatever happened ruined and polluted his mind and soul tremendously.

"The snake ass nigga I allowed in my circle and trusted with my life killed Kaze, gave my mother a raw bag of dope knowing it was going to kill her, robbed me for everything I had, and while I was locked up he slaughtered most of my crew and took over all my blocks. Then, the nigga bailed me out of jail and tried to murder me."

All Things eyes grew wide.

"If it wasn't for big unc I wouldn't even be here talking right now."

Real felt completely embarrassed telling his mentor how he slipped up. All Things managed to keep a straight face, but he was really flabbergasted and could not believe what he just heard.

"So you mean to tell me you ain't got nothing?"

"Nah, nothing. That's why I need you to throw me a couple of them things so I can get right back."

"How would you be able to get rid of the product if you don't have any soldiers nor blocks to move it on?" All Things questioned.

"I got a spot down south where my baby mom little brother and his team hustle at. They been begging me to come down there for the longest and supply them with some grade A shit. They ready to touch that real paper. I want Sal to role with me."

Wild Sal joined in.
"You don't have to go out of town to get ya money nephew. I shot that snake muhfucka right in the face. I guarantee you he bled to death in that car he rode off in."

Sal been laying his murder game down for years, and was very sure of his shot.

"No disrespect to ya aim big unc, but if he was able to run to that car the way he did it's a possibility that he's still alive. Even if he did bleed to death, his right hand man Low Down..."

Real noticed the puzzled look on Sal's face.

"The one that was driving," Real explained.

Sal quickly thought back to that night.

"The nigga loyal as hell to that snake, so he going to try his best to carry out whatever they had planned. He's also smarter and..."

"Them niggas probably think you dead, it'll be easy to kill em'!" Sal exclaimed.

"Yeah they probably do, but it's too much of a risk. I ain't got no bread stacked. I'd rather disappear for a while, get my paper back up, build another army, and then come back to Trenton to handle my handle. By that time Snake Eyes and his crew will be relaxed and off point. Especially if All Things can pull some of his political strings and make it look like I was murdered in the newspaper. We can have a closed casket..."

All Things cut Real off once he saw that his imagination was running too wild.

"We don't have to go through all of that. I'll have my hit squad from out of state come down here and wipe out their whole entire piece of shit movement."

Real began shaking his head in disagreement.

"Nah, this shit personal. That nigga did too much to me, I'm going to handle it myself."

After seeing Real's reaction, All Things understood and respected his young protege's wishes.

"Alright, it is what it is. Whatever you want to do just let me know and I'll make it happen."

All Things' mind was at ease knowing Real was smart enough not to lead himself or others to failure and destruction.

CHAPTER 4

Dynasty pulled out of the driveway with baby Zah Zah sitting quietly in her car seat. They were on their way to the train station. Real and Wild Sal secretly followed her in an all white tented out Buick, just in case Snake Eyes and his goons were lurking around in the area.

After making sure Dynasty and the baby boarded their train safely the two men drove down south with 10 keys of pure cocaine supplied by All Things. While on the road Real called his big sister Tadasia and informed her that he faked his death and was moving down south a few towns from where some of their family lived. Tadasia had already moved out of New Jersey, but Real still made sure his sister knew that he was in some very serious beef and that it was important for her not to go to Trenton under any circumstances.

Tayla, Dynasty, and J.J. were in the living room sitting on the long brown couch talking when Real and Wild Sal walked through the door. Real had a dark green duffle bag in his hand.

"There they go right there", Tayla said.

Tayla sat between her son and daughter, holding Zanyah feeding her a bottle of milk. This was the first time Tayla spent time with her granddaughter so she was very excited.

"It's about time y'all got here," Dynasty added.

"We got tired and pulled over to take a sleep break," Real explained.

J.J. nodded in acknowledgment to the other men in the house. Real noticed how excited Tayla was.

"What's up mom dukes."

"Hey son in law! I hope you just don't up and leave without telling anyone like you did last time. You damn near drove my daughter crazy!"

Dynasty snapped her teeth.

"He ain't almost drive nobody crazy. Mom stop lying to that boy."

Tayla looked at her daughter with a facial expression that said *Stop lying*.

"Nah, y'all ain't ever gotta worry about that happening again. Whenever I decide to make a quick run, your daughter will be the first to know."

J.J. was still looking at Sal. Real realized he never introduced them.

"Oh, I almost forgot. Kim and J.J. this my Uncle Sal, Uncle Sal that's Dynasty's mom Kim and her little brother J.J."

"How y'all doing, pleased to meet you." "It's nice to meet you too", Kim responded.

Kim remained cordial even though she couldn't help but wonder why Real would bring the rough looking man along with him to live.

Once everyone became acquainted with each other, it was time for Real and J.J. to speak about the business plan he had in mind. He

tapped J.J. on the shoulder. "Let me holla at you for a minute."

J.J. and Real walked towards the kitchen with Wild Sal following behind.

Real was exhausted mentally and his heart ached tremendously, but he knew exactly what he needed to do and was very determined to get it done. The men went down into the basement. Real flicked the light switch and everything became visible in the decked out basement. He picked up a large duffle bag and placed on the table.

"Grab a seat", Real directed.

Wild Sal and J.J sat down at the table, directly across from each other while Real remained at the head. Real opened the bag and pulled out a key of cocaine and placed it on the table. "Listen lil bro..."

Real noticed how wide J.J. eyes got. "Man look at me and listen!"

J.J. quickly shifted his attention back to Real.

"I kept my word by coming down here with the product, now it's your turn to keep your word by getting rid of it in a reasonable amount of time."

"Oh big bruh you ain't gotta worry about nothing. I'ma handle my handle, believe that", J.J. assured eagerly.
I wish this little nigga just be quiet and listen, Real thought to himself as he glanced at Wild Sal.

"You playing varsity now. If you really want to get rich I'm going to help you do it. All you have to do is stay true to your grind and remain loyal to me."

J.J. looked Real in his eyes and nodded his head indicating that he understood and agreed with what was being explained to him.

"Oh yeah, and most importantly I only exist to you and only you. I don't want any of these niggas down here to know who I am. Me and big unc gotta be as far under the radar as possible. Understand?" Real said making sure to emphasize every word.
"Yeah big bruh, I got you."

After Real outlined how he wanted things to move, J.J. took the kilo and rushed out of the house. He was on his way to the hood to get his grind on. Real was planning the ultimate takeover. In actuality he could have easily stretched an extra 800 grams out of every key that he had, but he knew that if he kept the first few keys pure the wind would blow all of the major money in the city his way. This would corner the market of every major hustler that couldn't provide the Grade A product Real supplied.

J.J. was smoking a dutch of some potent weed in the living room of his trap house. He was joined by Chris, a tall brown skin hustler with a low cut, and Mell who was dark skin and rocked a bald head. The three were close friends since elementary school, and did almost everything together. When J.J. told them about the new movement they didn't think twice about it, they were with it.

"Damn bruh, pass the weed", Chris said looking at J.J.

J.J. was in the middle of taking a long pull of the weed. He blew the smoke out of his mouth while looking back at Chris.
"Man you hitting the dutch last with that big ass bump

on ya lip. You ain't gonna have me walking around looking like I was eating frog pussy."

Mell burst in to laughter.
"Aww man, he said frog pussy. That fool silly as hell."

J.J. handed the smoke to Mell instead. Chris frowned his face up.
"Come on now, that shit ain't even that funny."

J.J. laughed knowing that he got under Chris' skin. "Ribbit! Ribbit! Ribbit!"

Mell began laughing even harder. Suddenly, someone started banging on the door.

KNOCK! KNOCK! KNOCK! For the last three days a countless amount of fiends and hustlers from the area were damn near kicking down the door in a rush to cop some of their potent product before it ran out.

"Get the door Chris", Mell directed, still laughing. "Nigga you get the door. Fuck you think this is." "You niggas must not want no money", J.J. interjected.

J.J. got up from the couch and went to the door. "Who is it?"
"It's Trey Dog", the person on the other side of the door answered.

J.J. glanced back at Chris and Mell before taking the lock off the door.

"What it is Dog", J.J. greeted, allowing the visitor to come in.

Trey Dog was a light skin husky fella that stood 6 feet tall with long curly hair he wore in 2 french braids. He grew up on the other side of town and was known for getting money and being the person everyone looked up to. So for someone of his caliber to be copping off of them said alot about J.J and his crew.

"You tell me, I'm hearing y'all the ones with the best coke in town. Let me get a hundred and fifty of them thangs", Trey Dog ordered.

Trey Dog would have normally purchased more, but he wanted to see how good the product was first.

J.J. and his crew's hustling procedure was to take turns on each sale, and it wasn't on J.J. But, being that he was the only one that had the amount Trey Dog was looking for he took it.

"Damn bruh, you just in time. That's all I got left."

J.J. walked over to the raggedy couch, dug his hand in the ripped cushion, and pulled out a clear plastic bag filled with coke along with a black digital scale. He went through the

process of weighing the bag of coke, showing Trey that it was the exact amount of cocaine he requested.
"You see it?"

"Yeah I see it."

The two made their exchange.

J.J. was ready to see Real so he could get more work. He thought about giving Real the money he owed the day before, but he decided to wait until he sold every crumb of coke. His plan was to be also be able to flip his whole hand in the process.

KNOCK! KNOCK! KNOCK!

"Who is it", Dynasty yelled.

Kim was on the couch holding the baby so she was unable to answer the door. Dynasty looked out the peephole before unlocking the door.

"Where Real at?" J.J asked, stepping inside.

"He upstairs", Dynasty replied before returning back in to the kitchen.
"What's up mom."
"Hey son", Kim replied.

J.J. went upstairs and walked down the hallway to the last door where he knocked lightly.

"Come in", Real answered.

J.J. opened the door and stepped inside of the bedroom. Real was sitting up in his king size bed sipping on a pint of Henny, watching the camera footage of his old crew and Snake Eyes when they were in Miami stunting on his 18th birthday. He had been studying the video for the last 3 days. The fire within him burned uncontrollably as he watched the fake love shown by Snake Eyes, who was secretly plotting and scheming the whole time. It gave Real the driving force that was going to help him climb from the bottom to the top again. Where he would cut off the head of the snake that bit him.

"Whats good?" Real greeted lazily, never taking his eyes off the tv screen.

Real was still drained from his mind replaying the same scenes. J.J. took a seat on the edge of the bed. "Some more work, that's what's good."

J.J. placed a bag full of cash on the bed. He finally noticed Real's bloodshot eyes and could tell something was really bothering him.

"You alright?"

"Yeah, I'm good."

"You sure?"

"Yeah. You a day early", Real changed the subject.

"I guess I ain't keep my word. I should've said three days."

J.J. grinned and tried to lighten up the mood. "Sike naw, that's the money I owe you, plus 30 stacks I want to spend. I'm trying to come up."

Real began to lighten up after hearing J.J. getting down to business. It's not that he slept on J.J.'s hustling ability, but he damn sure wasn't expecting him to be on his grizzly grind like this. *Everything is going to go just how I planned*, Real thought to himself feeling confident. Once Real counted the cash, he grabbed three kilo's of cocaine and passed them off to J.J.

CHAPTER 5

The treacherous Snake Eyes wasn't your ordinary snake, he was a king cobra with deadly poisonous venom pumping through his veins. He knew that once he murdered Kamikaze, Real would be one of the first people to show up at the hospital. Snake Eyes arranged to have three of his soldiers outside waiting for Real so they could erase him out of the picture. But things didn't go as planned, forcing Snake Eyes to immediately come up with a different strategy.

After watching two of his men get laid down, Snake Eyes couldn't risk the third man getting away and running his lips about the mission. And with Real surviving the hit, it was only a matter of time for the word to get back to him. The only choice was for Snake Eyes to murder the third gunman, pretending to come to Real's aid. Snake Eyes' move was guaranteed to change the dynamic of he and Real's relationship. Real would see him as a loyal supporter that had his best interest at heart, especially after Snake Eyes pretended to go out of his way to find out who killed Kaze.

There was no doubt Snake Eyes' strategic chess game was vicious! He targeted Fletcho and marked him as Kaze's murderer just to get him out the way. Fletcho was the only competition as far as drug money was concerned on Snake Eyes' side of Trenton. Once Real unknowingly handled Snake Eyes' dirty work, he used the high level of trust he gained to his advantage. He was able to cleverly talk Real into giving him the coke for almost the exact same price he was purchasing it for, and he also talked him into forming an alliance that would take over the entire city.

Snake Eyes was able to get his money up and build his army, but never got Real to introduce him to the connect. Once he found his own plug, Snake Eyes decided that it was time to crush Real completely!

Snake Eyes sat in the back row of his Black Escalade truck using his money machine to count the cash from the green duffle bag he just picked up from one of his workers. He wrapped the money up in rubber band stacks and stashed them neatly. Low Down cruised through the small suburban towns of South Jersey bobbing his head and singing to the music of new rap artist Carde'l.

"I does this, I love this, this what I live for!"

Low Down reached out to a few of his peoples in Burlington, Mount Holly, and Willingboro to let them know he had grade A work for a decent price. Snake Eyes takeover expansion was taking it's course.

"I can't even count ssstraight with that loud ass musssic on. Turn that ssshit down!" Snake Eyes demanded.

When Wild Sal shot Snake Eyes in the face the bullet came out of the side of his mouth and pierced his tongue, causing him to permanently talk with a hiss like the snake he truly was.

"We got too much money in this car to be driving around like we having a party in thisss muhfucka!"

Low Down glanced back at Snake Eyes. "Aight man damn. I heard you."

Low Down pulled inside a small housing complex and spotted his younger cousin T.J. leaning up against a green pick-up truck. BEEP! Low Down pressed down on the car horn as he pulled up in front of him. "What's good big cuz", T.J. greeted as he got inside the truck.

"You already know cuzzo. That paper spread", Low Down responded.

"Man where the money at?" Snake Eyes abruptly interrupted.

"It's right here", T.J. assured.

As Snake Eyes reached to grab the money bag from T.J., he noticed a fine ass female walking a small fluffy white dog. She was a red bone with long hair and a body that was out of this world.

"Damn who that?"

Snake Eyes continued to watch her booty jiggle with every step she took. T.J. smirked when he saw the familiar looking young lady. "That's Kiki. She bad as hell ain't she."

T.J. chuckled because he knew that Kiki was an 18 year old virgin that did not like drug dealers. As far as he was concerned, Snake Eyes didn't have chance.

Snake Eyes opened the door and hopped out. Kiki was only a few feet away.

"A yo Kiki, ssslow down", he hissed.

Snake Eyes began walking towards her. Kiki was slightly startled after turning around to see the unfamiliar man coming her way. She kept walking. *Who the hell is that, and how do he know my name?* Kiki thought to herself.

"Oh ssso you gonna act like you don't hear me huh."

Snake Eyes began speed walking behind her. The little dog began barking and tried to bite the intruder when he got closer. Snakes Eyes found the dog comical. "Mirabella calm down", Kiki demanded calming the dog immediately.

"You ain't gotta wild out on little Mirabella like that. Shit, if I was walking with sssomebody asss fly asss you and nigga tried to holla I would be acting the sssame way."

Snake Eyes spoke with charm, trying to make a good first impression. Kiki giggled as she looked Snake Eyes up and down, taking in the extravagant blue diamond earrings and expensive clothes and fresh sneakers he had on.

"Boy how you know my name?"
"When you a duffle bag boy you know everything."
"Umm, duffle bag boy huh." "Yeah, duffle bag boy", Snake Eyes shot back.

Kiki started to blush. Snake Eyes pulled a thick wad of cash from his pocket and held it up in front of her face. Kiki's eyes grew wide in amazement, she tried her best to play it off and keep her composure.

"Boy where you get all that money from?"

"This right here? Girl this ain't no money. Here take it."

Snake Eyes tried to hand the money over to Kiki. She looked at the crispy hundred dollar bills, and then in to his slanted eyes.

"Take it. Why you acting like you ssscared of money or sssomething."
"But I don't even know you."
"Just call me Duffle Bag Boy. Anytime you want sssomething call me, I'm giving you the paper ssso you can get whatever you want. No matter what it isss."

"You funny."
"I'm dead serious. Now give me your number and take this money and go shopping."

Kiki finally gave in and took the money, giving Snake Eyes her number.

After Low Down and Snake Eyes left Willingboro they drove straight to the graveyard in Ewing, New Jersey so they could do their monthly ritual. Snake Eyes handed Low Down the fifth of Henny before climbing out of the truck. He began walking through the cemetery with a grim smirk on his face. There was something about the gloomy and morbid vibe of this place that made his adrenaline rush and manhood rock hard.

"We meet again", Snake Eyes said through his wicked laugh.

Snake Eyes approached the headstones of Kaze and Real's mother Nyla. Their headstones were two of the largest displays in the entire cemetery, and they were both adorned with colorful flowers. Snake Eyes hog spit on both of their graves before he unzipped his pants and pissed all over the vibrant flowers. He intentionally drunk plenty of Henny and held his piss for hours just so he could be able to fill their grave sites with his foul smelling urine.

After doing all of the terrible things to Real, Snake Eyes' monthly ritual was the ultimate get high. It added to the victorious feeling that traveled through his body when he read about Real's demise in the Trenton Times several months ago. The newspaper confirmed Real's death and also stated that because of his unfortunate financial issues, the family did not have enough money for a funeral so the slain man had to be cremated.

"Ahhh", Snake Eyes groaned, feeling relieved as the last bit of piss left his body.

Meanwhile, Qadeesha was walking up about 20 feet away with 2 dozen of fresh red roses in her hand. She spotted the man standing over top of Kaze's grave with his penis in his hand. She was in shock and stopped dead in her tracks.

"Who the hell!" She exclaimed in disbelief.

A fiery rage began to burn through the center of Qadeesha's body. She would visit Kaze's grave every three weeks and always thought that the cats that roamed the graveyard were responsible for the dead flowers and foul smelling odor. Now she was witnessing the real perpetrator. Qadeesha scanned the grass until she spotted a brick on the ground a few feet away. She grabbed the brick from off the ground and stormed towards Snake Eyes who still had his back turned.

"Get the fuck away from my man!"

Qadeesha threw the brick as hard as she could, cracking Snake Eyes in the back of the head.
"Ahhgg!", he groaned in agony.

The blow caused Snake Eyes to stumble back. He placed his hand over the bloody gash in the back of his head. The intense pain caused him to become just as furious as Qadeesha. Snake Eyes was kind of dizzy, but he managed to stay on his feet and quickly turned around to see who his attacker was. Qadeesha charged at him, screaming to the top of her lungs. Snake Eyes quickly side stepped and hit her with a wild right hook that landed directly on her chin. "Agghh!" She yelled in pain as she fell to the ground.

The side of Qadeesha's face swelled up instantly.

"Bitch!" Snake Eyes growled.
Snake Eyes stood over top of Qadeesha and began stomping her relentlessly. She began screaming and balled up her body in an attempt to block the forceful blows that were coming back to back. Through all of the commotion, Qadeesha still managed to get a good look at his face. She recognized him.

CHAPTER 6

Wild Sal sat on one side of the living room while Real and Dynasty sat on the other. Zanyah played with her toys on the floor. There was a tense feeling in the room. Dynasty got the news from Qadeesha about the horrible incident that took place between her and Snake Eyes. She was still crying her eyes out and knew that the news had her man to the point of no return.

Real sat close beside Dynasty as tears burned his bloodshot red eyes. The energy he felt was so powerful that everyone in the living room could feel it beaming off him. *I'm driving back to Trenton tonight and I'm going to murder that snake ass nigga wherever I see him. Fuck that! He think I'm dead anyway. It's gonna be easy...Nah, I gotta fall back and keep my composure and stick to the plan.* The thoughts were racing through Real's mind. His scarred mind and aching heart played tug of war with each other. He was so tempted to get in his car and drive back to his city, but he knew in order for everything to go exactly how he wanted he had to follow his plan precisely.

"Da da!"
Zanyah crawled over to her father and began pulling on his pants. Real looked down at his daughter holding out her arms with a wide smile on her face showing her new two bottom teeth. He looked into her innocent green eyes and the tension immediately began to subside. Zanyah was his pride and joy, and the sight of her always made him feel good inside. She was his happy thought.

"Not right now Zah Zah. Daddy got a lot on his mind", Dynasty said.

Dynasty was about to pick Zanyah up, but Real stopped her.

"She good", Real said.

Real took his daughter in his arms knowing that holding her was probably the only thing that could calm his nerves. Zanyah was excited to be held by her dad, she began to playfully jump up and down in her father's

lap. Real couldn't help but to laugh and play along.

About an hour had passed and Real was still holding Zanyah who was drinking a bottle while dozing off in his lap. Dynasty was still sitting next to her man, and Wild Sal was in the basement. Dynasty stared at Real as he looked in to his daughter's face. She wanted to ask him earlier if Qadeesha can come to stay with them after she got out of the hospital. But after sensing the scorching hot vibe emanating from Real she told herself she would wait for him to cool off a little bit. That time was now.

"Baby can Qadeesha come down here and stay with us for a few weeks."

Real shook his head in disapproval.

"I already told you I don't want nobody in the city to know that I'm alive."

Dynasty snapped her teeth.

"She ain't gonna let nobody know you alive. She's family and she's gonna be down here with us."

"I know she not because she ain't coming down here."

Real knew how Dynasty felt about her cousin and he wanted to tell her it was alright for Qadeesha to live with them, but knowing how she could be sometimes he couldn't risk the chance of her running her mouth to anyone. Dynasty tried her best to remain calm.

"Well I'm going back to Trenton for a few weeks to spend some time with her then." "No you..."

Before Real could finish his sentence, someone began knocking on the front door. Dynasty got up from the couch to answer it.

"Who is it!"

"It's J.J."

Dynasty let her little brother in and walked back to the couch and sat down. J.J. had a duffle bag in his hand.

"What it is big sis, Real."

"Same ol' bullshit", Dynasty replied sounding depressed and fed up.

J.J. noticed the sad tone in his sister's voice, and the disturbed look on Real's face.

"What's wrong?"

"Some nigga put his hands on Qadeesha to the point where she's in the hospital."

Dynasty wanted to give her brother just enough information, not knowing if Real wanted him to know the full details of the story.

"Word up? Who was it, her boyfriend?"

Dynasty looked at Real waiting for him to give her the approval to keep talking. Real gently handed the baby over to Dynasty and stood up from the couch. "Nah, it wasn't her boyfriend", Real said.

Real noticed the anger that was building up in J.J. "Who the hell was it then? Y'all want to take a ride down there?"

J.J. couldn't understand why they were holding back. He might have been country but he damn sure wasn't slow, and he definitely didn't play when it came to his family. Even though Qadeesha was a distant cousin that he didn't know too well, he still was ready to take that ride to Jersey and bust a nigga ass for her.

"It's a long story that you'll know about when the time comes. Right now, we need to focus on business", Real stated.

J.J. still had a confused look on his face.

"Oh don't worry, things are definitely going to get taken care of. Trust me. Come in the kitchen", Real said.

J.J. stood there for a few seconds not knowing what to say before eventually following Real.

Real took a seat at the table, J.J. handed him the bag. "That's 250k straight cash."

Real unzipped the bag to examine the stacks of cash that were neatly wrapped in rubber bands. *Aight, now it's time to get shit moving*, Real thought to himself. Things were going better than Real planned. J.J. went from selling one key in three of four days, to moving 3 or 4 keys in one day.

Real's next move for his crew was to start spreading coke from town to town until he supplied majority of the state. But, before they could do that there were two areas in J.J.'s town that still had to be put in the cocaine choke hold.

"Aight look, I want you to go holla at Lazy C and Peezo. We got pure coke for cheap and whatever they cop we gonna front 'em half of whatever they cop on consignment. All they got to do is keep spending they money with us and nobody else", Real explained.

Real knew about everyone and everything that went on in town, and the beauty of it all was that no one even knew he existed.

J.J. grinned and nodded his head in agreement. "That's what it is then. I'm 'bout to go handle that right now."

J.J. got up and walked out the kitchen.

"I'm about to put 10 of them things together for you so come right back", Real said.

J.J. got in his vehicle and pulled off, heading straight to Lazy-C's trap spot. He knew the two potential clients very well so he figured they would be more than willing to take full advantage of the proposition.

KNOCK! KNOCK! KNOCK! J.J. stood at the front door of the trap house hoping Lazy C was inside. "Who is it!" a deep voice asked from inside.

Lazy C must have looked through the peep hole because within seconds the door was unlocked and opened. A smile came across J.J.'s face after seeing Lazy C standing in the doorway.

"What's going on with you big bruh", J.J. greeted.

The two slapped hands with each other. Lazy C was a short and chubby brown skin young hustler, with a low clean cut. He had a chipped front tooth and droopy eyes which is why everyone called him Lazy C. Not to mention he was also lazy as hell. The only time he got motivated was when it was time to grind that paper up and count it. But then again he always did that while plopped on the couch at his hustling spot.

"Same ol' same ol'. What's going on with you, ain't seen you in a nice little minute", Lazy C responded.

Lazy C was under the assumption that J.J. came to spend some money with him. Before Real came in to the picture J.J. used to spend his money with Lazy C whenever Peezo ran out of work.

"Come in", Lazy C stated.

He locked the door and started walking towards the kitchen.
"Follow me", he said.

As they walked through the living room, J.J. nodded at the young man sitting on the couch who was holding a chrome .357 Magnum in his lap.

Once they got in the kitchen, Lazy C opened the cabinet above the sink and grabbed a digital scale and a plastic bag filled halfway with cocaine. He placed everything on the kitchen table.

"So what you trying to spend?"

The two were standing face to face.

"Nah bruh I ain't come over here for that. I came to holla at you about some other important business."

Lazy C raised a curious eyebrow. "About what?"
"Let's sit down first", J.J. stated.

The two sat down, and J.J. explained the proposal just as Real explained it to him. It felt kind of awkward to Lazy C to have someone he was supplying a few months ago approach him with a business offer on such a high level. But despite his emotions, Lazy C knew deep down inside that offers like this were rare. He put his pride aside, and agreed to get down with the movement.

After everything was settled with Lazy C, J.J. made his way to Peezo's side of town. When J.J. walked on the porch he noticed someone peaking through the blinds in the downstairs window. Before he could begin knocking, the door swung open.

"What's up stranger", Peezo greeted with a wide smile, revealing a mouth full of gold teeth.

Peezo had a dark brown skin complexion with shoulder length box braids. He also had thick eye brows that matched his full beard. Peezo had his hood on smash, but was somewhat of a tyrant. He talked to his workers any kind of way, he didn't pay them well, and he beat them up whenever they spoke their mind. No one in his organization liked him and wanted him out of the way, but they were all too scared to do something about it.

"Come in and lock the door behind you", Peezo ordered.

Peezo strolled over to the cream leather couch and took a seat. J.J. walked in the living room but remained standing.

"Sit down nigga. Fuck you standing over top of me for", Peezo ordered.

J.J. finally sat down. Peezo removed the blunt of kush from his ear and sparked up.
"So what made you come through after all this time. You fell off or something? What, you was too prideful to come holla at me like you used to back in the good ol' days?" Peezo asked blowing a thick cloud of smoke in the air.

"Nah, it ain't nothing like that dawg. I came over here to let you know that I got that white girl for cheap and I'm willing to front you half of whatever you cop." J.J. offered with a smirk on his face.

Peezo stared in to J.J.'s eyes for a few seconds, then threw his head back and burst in to a loud laughter. He couldn't believe the comical shit he had just heard. Here you have it, J.J. a small time hustler from across the other side of town whom never served a quarter kilo of cocaine, standing in front of you saying that he could front half of whatever.

You gotta be fucking kidding me, Peezo thought to himself. "Awww man. You shot the hell out lil bruh."

Peezo was still trying to control his laugh. "Man you must be high. Shit whatever you've been smoking I need some of that shit. Word up."

Peezo took another pull on of the kush. J.J. frowned his face up, feeling offended. *Oh this clown ass nigga think I'm a joke*, he said to himself.

"I ain't high nigga!"

J.J. reached in his pocket and pulled out a 100 gram pack of cocaine and tossed it in to Peezo's lap.
"I got the best coke in town, and I can cover whatever order you put in."

J.J. didn't care how Peezo would react. He was one of the few dudes that wasn't afraid of Peezo, especially now that he had a fortified movement and a whole bunch of paper stacks backing him up.

"Thats just a sample for you to serve the fiends. See how they like it", J.J. said cockily.

Peezo now had a surprised look on his face. He looked down at the plastic bag, picked it up, and opened it. *Damn this really do look like some good shit*, he thought to himself. Peezo stuck his finger inside and rubbed it on his gums.

"Ummm, this some grade A shit right here man. Where you get this shit from?"

"Is you with the movement or what?" J.J. shot back. "You better watch your tone lil nigga. Who the fuck you think you talking to!"

J.J. breathed heavily out of his nose, trying his best to keep his composure.
"Man like I said, are you with the movement or what?"

I know if this lil piss head gave me all this powder for a sample, he must really have it how he say he got it, Peezo thought. He pondered for a few seconds, not sure of what he was going to do. "Nah, I'm good", he stated in a hostile tone.

Peezo's foolish pride wouldn't allow him to purchase work off of someone he considered a small time hustler. He was the one looking out for J.J. whenever he fell off.

"Say no more. You can keep that lil punk ass 100 grams", J.J. said as he made his way out of the house.

As soon as the front door slammed shut, Peezo went over to the window to look out the blinds.
"Uh huh. I'm gonna find out where ya lil punk ass getting ya coke from", he said to himself in a low menacing tone.

Peezo waited for J.J. to pull off before he rushed out of the house. He climbed in his black Taurus and started following J.J. J.J. finally pulled up in front of Real and Dynasty's house. Peezo slowed down and parked his car far down the street.

J.J. walked on the porch and began knocking on the door. Peezo was able to get a glimpse of Real's face when he opened the door to let J.J. in. *That must be the plug right there,* he thought.

Not even two minutes passed before J.J. was walking back out the house with a duffle bag in his hand. Real and Dynasty walked out with him. Real was about to drop Dynasty off at the train station. He was tired of hearing her mouth and didn't want Qadeesha to come

down and find out he was really alive. His only choice was to allow his baby mother to go back to Trenton for a few weeks to comfort and spend time with her favorite cousin.

CHAPTER 7

Snake Eyes waited impatiently in the overcrowded clinic lobby. *Damn man, I wish these muhfuckas hurry up and call me,* he thought to himself. He began looking around at the other people waiting. There were old, young, and middle aged sick people all around him. *Damn it look like everybody 'bout to die in this bitch.*

Snake Eyes' body had been feeling unusual lately. He had uncontrollable diarrhea for the last week and a half, and aches and pains that caused him to feel very weak. He decided to set up an appointment to get checked out for possible diseases. Testing for diseases was always standard when coming to a clinic like this. They always assumed it was a high possibility that their patients, especially of a certain age, were exposed to some type of STD.

Snake Eyes started coughing uncontrollably, causing some of the people in the waiting area to turn and stare.

"Are you alright sir?" An elderly woman asked. "Yeah, I'm good", Snake Eyes replied in between coughs using his hand to cover his mouth.

After another fifteen minutes of waiting, a short brown skin female nurse walked in to the lobby. Everyone stopped what they were doing and put all of their focus on her, in hopes that their names would get called next.

"Mr. Shawn Cross", the nurse called out.
"It's about fucking time", Snake Eyes murmured.

Snake Eyes rose from his seat and began following the nurse. Once they entered the examine room, he quietly closed the door behind him and sat down in the seat beside the nurse's desk.

"Okay Mr. Cross we're going to run a series of tests today. One of the tests will be for HIV", the nurse stated.

Snake Eyes listened and watched while the nurse put on her gloves and prepared the needle and tubes for the blood work. Snake Eyes had unprotected sex with almost every single woman he slid inside of, so the thought of being tested for HIV caused his heart to race. *Damn man, I hope I ain't got that shit*, he said to himself as he began to regret his reckless lifestyle.

"Alright Mr. Cross, this is a rapid test that will test you for the AIDS/HIV virus. Just hold it in your mouth on the side of your cheek."

Snake Eyes followed her directions.

"For the blood work I need you to extend your arm for me please."

The nurse rubbed an alcohol swab on the middle of his arm and stuck him with the needle. The pinch caused Snake Eyes to tense up. He watched his blood slowly fill the different vials the nurse attached to the needle.

In a matter of seconds everything was done. The nurse cleaned up his arm, and disposed of the needle. She put the blood samples and the HIV test in a container.

"Alright hold tight. I'll be right back", she assured before walking out of the examine room door.

Snake Eyes sat all the way back in his seat and started staring at the ceiling. He wanted to know the outcome of the test results, but at the same time he didn't want to know if he had HIV. The thought of it was too depressing for him.

After about 15 minutes, a white male doctor came back in the room. The sound of the door closing snapped

Snake Eyes from out of his trance. *Who the fuck is he?* Snake Eyes thought.

"Hello Mr. Cross, I'm Dr. Moore and I am here to discuss your test results. That's the one thing our nurses don't do."

The doctor took a seat and began to open Snake Eyes' file. Snake Eyes' breath got caught in his throat as he anticipated the next words to come out of the doctor's mouth.

"Mr. Cross, I am very sorry but the results of your HIV test came back positive."

The doctor paused, waiting to see his patient's reaction. Snake Eyes leaned forward and put his face in the palms of his hands. He stayed in this position for several seconds. *Damn, I really got that shit*, he thought. He couldn't help but wish he was dreaming as the feeling of depression consumed him.

The doctor began to explain the next steps on how he was to care for himself and how to avoid spreading the disease to others. But before he could finish explaining Snake Eyes bolted up from his seat. "Fuck!" He yelled before storming out of the room.

During the next few weeks Snake Eyes went on a complete rampage. He had unprotected sex with at least 40 different women. Snake Eyes didn't discriminate when it came to who he had sex with. From very young girls to women old enough to be somebody's grandmother, he screwed them all. He told himself *fuck it*, since one of the dirty bitches he fucked raw gave it to him he was going to give it to as many people as possible - until the day he dropped dead. Finding a victim was never hard since he was a certified trick and blew money like it grew on trees. Snake Eyes was no longer just a snake with a poisonous bite, he had a poisonous dick too.

Snake Eyes was laid up in the king size bed watching Kiki as she came out of the hotel bathroom.
"Damn", he said under his breath in amazement.

Kiki was completely naked, exposing her high yellow curvaceous frame. She seductively walked towards him with her thick thighs and perky breast jiggling with every step she took. The shopping sprees sponsored by Snake Eyes were finally about to pay off. Kiki allowed his charming words and long money to cloud her vision, which led her right to the Holiday Inn.

She believed that Snake Eyes wanted to be with her and only her, so she thought that he was worthy of being the one to take her virginity. Little did she know she was about to make the worst mistake of her life.

Snake Eyes had a smirk on his face, his eyes were still glued on Kiki while she climbed inside the bed. The innocent young lady got under the covers and cuddled up underneath him. She began rubbing on his boney chest and noticed a very interesting looking tattoo of a king cobra with dark red eyes. It started from the top of his chest and ended near his navel.

"Oh my goodness! I know that tattoo hurt didn't it", she asked looking Snake Eyes in the face.
"Nah, after a few minutesss everything went numb and I ain't feel a thing", Snake Eyes responded.

His penis began to harden so he removed the sheets, revealing his skinny body. Kiki gasped at the sight of him. *Oh shit, he about to stick that big thing up in me*, she thought to herself in shock staring down at his 10 inch throbbing manhood. Snake Eyes began stroking his dick after he noticed the stunned look on her face. "Calm down baby, it ain't gonna hurt. I'ma take it nice and ssslow", he states smoothly hoping his words comforted her.

Snake Eyes sat up and rolled over on top of her. He made his way down in between her thick yellow thighs that were already spread apart. Snake Eyes began to devour her neatly shaven honey pot like a wild beast that hadn't eaten in weeks.

"Ahh shit...damn...", Kiki moaned out loud.

She grabbed hold to Snake Eyes' long corn rows as tight as she could as her entire body began to quiver.
"I'm cummin!"

Kiki was having back to back orgasms. When Snake Eyes got tired of eating her pussy, he bent Kiki over doggy style. He slid his unprotected manhood inside of her tight wetness and began beating it up from the back. In 15 minutes he exploded, spitting his deadly venom inside of the former virgin. They were both exhausted and fell asleep next to each other.

The next morning Snake Eyes dropped Kiki off and picked up Low Down from his house and began touring the town. Even though Snake Eyes knocked Real out of the box and was notoriously labeled as the new king of the city, he still made it his duty every once in a while to blatantly let it be known who ran things. He would pop up unexpectedly on the different blocks that he owned just to boss his workers around. Sometimes he even went to the extent of pistol whipping or shooting them if they weren't conducting business to his standards. This behavior was only done because Snake Eyes knew nobody would dare fuck with him. Peezo ain't have shit on the way he tyrannized.

Snake Eyes grew tired of driving so he let Low Down take the wheel.

"Damn bruh, I need sssomething to drink. Go to the liquor ssstore on the boulevard."

Low Down was leaned back in the driver's seat bobbing his head to Carte'l. *Certified dope boy, certified dope boy. Stacks so fat rubber bands can't hold my shit.* Once they made it to the liquor store, Snake Eyes hopped out and went inside.

"Let me get a fifth of that black Henny", he ordered.

There was a chubby Hispanic lady standing behind the counter. Snake Eyes pulled a 50 dollar bill from his pocket and handed it to her. The lady handed him his bottle and tried to give him his change.

"You can keep it", Snake Eyes said making his way out of the store.

As soon as he hit the pavement he stopped dead in his tracks.
"Oh ssshit, I know that ain't..."

Snake Eyes' lustful eyes grew wide. He was completely flabbergasted at the sight of Dynasty walking out of the laundromat across the street. Snake Eyes had been on somewhat of a hunt for Dynasty ever since he read about Real's death in the newspaper. He could never find her, and always wondered where she disappeared to. But now, after all this time there she was.

Low Down rolled the car window down and stuck his head out.
"You see ol' girl over there huh."

Low Down knew his partner in crime was cuckoo crazy over Dynasty, and found it quite amusing. Snake Eyes winked at Low Down before walking across the street.

He really fell deeply in love with Dynasty the first time he saw her at Kaze's funeral. And since the only man that stood in his way was gone, he figured she was fair game.

Dynasty was putting a bag of clothes in the back seat of the car she rented so her back was turned with Snake Eyes approached her. "Dynasty."

Startled, she quickly turned to see Snake Eyes standing behind her. Dynasty turned around to face him. *Oh shit! What to do? What to say?* She asked herself in a panic while trying to keep her cool at the same time. *Calm down Dynasty and think.*

Snake Eyes could sense Dynasty's uneasiness and smirked.
"Damn baby ease up. I ain't gonna bite... unlesss you tell me to", he hissed. *She probably know I killed her bitch ass babydad*, he thought while looking into her green eyes.

"But anyway, where you been at? I ain't ssseen you sssince the day I dropped that bread off for Real'sss bail. I tried to find you after I found out he got killed ssso I could help pay for the funeral, but you were no where to be found", he explained sounding very sincere.

"I just had to get away for a little bit. It was too much going on", Dynasty responded noticing the lustful glow in his eyes.

"I hope you know if you need anything, no matter what it isss, all you have to do isss give me a call."

After murdering Real and robbing him for all of his money Snake Eyes knew that Dynasty was vulnerable and in desperate need for money. Now was the time to exploit her weakness.

Dynasty just stood there in silence for a few seconds. *What to do! What to say!* She kept repeating to herself.

Then it finally kicked in. *This stupid snake ass nigga think I'm weak and fucked up out here. I got something for his ass.* A deviously sexy smile appeared on her face, and she began to lick her lips.

"How am I gonna call when I don't even have your number. I lost my old phone", she told him.

Snake Eyes was getting a hard on just from the sound of her sweet voice and the sight of her tongue.
"Grab your phone so I can give it to you", he said.

Dynasty pulled out her phone. "What is it?"

Snake Eyes called out his number. Dynasty looked down and noticed the bulge in his pants.
"Ummm, looks like you ready to get yourself in to something you can't handle", she stated flirtatiously.

A bashful smile appeared on his face. "Something I can't handle. Ha, that's funny."

The two said their goodbyes and went their separate ways.

CHAPTER 8

Real sat in the empty house staring at the wall in deep thought. His mind raced back to when he was 10 years old sitting in the living room of his mother's house watching tv when all of a sudden the front door swung open and Nyla stormed in holding the side of her swollen face.

"I got something for this muhfucka", she said under her breath.

Nyla walked to the kitchen.

"Mom what's wrong?"Real asked.

Real was worried about his mother so he got up from the floor and followed her. Once inside the kitchen Real watched as Nyla pulled a huge ice pick from behind the refrigerator.

"Mom, what's going on?"

Nyla could barely hear or pay attention to her son, she was too furious. Without saying a word, she left out of the kitchen and back out the house leaving the front door wide open. Real was so afraid for his mother that he ran out behind her barefoot and dressed in pajamas. He ran off the porch and down the street. It was 95 degrees outside so the hot pavement burned the bottom of young Real's feet.

Nyla finally made it to the end of the corner where Real noticed the well known dope dealer K.O. standing. K.O. was a tall, slim, light skin young man with a shiny bald head that had a huge scar on it. He stood there shirtless with his back turned to Nyla. Just before she got close enough to stab him, K.O. turned to see Nyla rushing towards him with the ice pick in her hand. He must have heard her footsteps as she crept up.

"Oh shit!" K.O. exclaimed.

His heart skipped a beat as he took off running around the corner.

"Oh don't run now muhfucka!" Nyla growled chasing behind him swinging her weapon.

"Mom!", Real panicked.

Not knowing what to do Real took off running behind Nyla. All three of them ran up a long and slanted side street.

As soon as K.O. got a nice distance from Nyla, he spotted a long thick piece of wood on the sidewalk and immediately tried to grab it. It was so heavy that he struggled to pick it up. Nyla was so consumed with rage that she didn't see K.O. pick up the large log. When she approached K.O. he threw the heavy log as hard as he could.

The make-shift weapon crashed against Nyla's skull, splitting her head to the white meat.
"Aghh!!!" She groaned.

With her ice-pick in hand, Nyla fell backwards and hit the hard concrete. The crimson red blood began to pour like a running faucet from her open wound. Real's innocent eyes watched the horrific scene and was devastated.

"Mom!" He yelled from the top of his lungs.

With tears in his eyes Real ran over to his mother's aid. But before he could make it to her, Nyla rushed up off the ground and charged K.O. like she was a raging bull.
"What the fuck!" K.O. exclaimed.

He took a few steps backwards before turning around and taking off again. After she saw the large amount of blood coming from her head, Nyla realized she would soon lose the strength she needed to catch up to K.O. She turned back around and walked towards the house. Real was still crying as he walked with his mother, trying to avoid stepping on glass and rocks. Once they made it back to the house, Nyla called a family member to take her to the hospital.

Real finished his trip down memory lane, causing his heart to yearn for revenge. After seeing K.O. crack his mother in the head, Real made a vow to himself that when he got older he was going to murder K.O. for what he did. Living the fast life and being caught up in so much over the years, the promise he made to himself slipped his mind. *I bet that bitch ass nigga out there still slinging dope*, Real said to himself.

Real grabbed his chrome Colt 45 handgun from in between the couch cushion and walked out of the front door. He climbed in his truck and pulled off. Real was on his way to visit his aunt who lived two towns away. He wanted to see how she was doing, but most importantly he was planning to live up to the silent vow he made to himself 9 years ago at the tender age of ten.

Real rode around the town in his all black tinted out pick up truck for five hours. He thought about how everything was going to play out, and didn't want to be too suspicious. He knew his family was aware of him witnessing what K.O. did to his mother, so he didn't want to pop up out of the blue before or after K.O. was murdered.

Real told himself the only way he was going to visit his family is if he couldn't find K.O.

He searched everywhere he thought K.O. would be, but couldn't find him anywhere. "Fuck man, this bitch ass nigga must've moved or something", Real said to himself.

This was the point in which Real decided he would pay his Aunt Tasha a visit.

Real pulled up on the long street where his aunt lived and parked in front of her big white and blue house. Just before getting out of the car he spotted an older looking bald headed man stepping off a porch several houses down. The man approached a dark skin elderly woman who handed him something. From the looks of it he was serving an addict.

"That look like that bitch ass nigga right there", Real said while squinting his eyes.

He pulled out the parking spot and drove towards the house.
"Yeah that's him."

Real slowly drove pass the house and noticed the huge scar on the back of K.O.'s head who was now walking back to the porch. His adrenaline began rushing at the sight of his prey.

"Um hum, I'm about to tear his ass up", he uttered in a menacing tone.

Real parked on the street around the corner from the house K.O. was trapping from. He pulled his black hoodie over his head and climbed out of his vehicle. Real began walking down the empty street, tucking his hand in his front hoodie pocket. He tightly wrapped his hand around his weapon. The closer he got to the corner the more his heart rate increased in anticipation. He was so close to shedding his enemy's blood he could taste it on the tip of his tongue.

Just before Real was about to turn the corner, he heard the loud sound of a cell phone ringing causing him to immediately stop in his tracks. He put his back up against the wall of an abandoned house, then sneakily peeked around the corner. Real saw K.O. walking towards his direction.

"Oh shit", Real whispered to himself.

He quickly dipped his head back and pulled out his weapon. K.O. was talking on the phone. Real timed his voice as it got louder and louder with every step. If only he knew that death was literally waiting for him around the corner.

Suddenly, Real swung around the corner with his chrome Colt 45 drawn. K.O. was caught by surprise and gasped, throwing his hands up in the air. His eyes grew extremely wide in fear. With each slow backwards step K.O took, Real would take a step forward.

"Please man..."

Before K.O. could finish his sentence Real let off four shots, striking him twice in each knee cap. K.O. yelled out in agony as he spun around and forcefully fell to the ground. K.O. was leaving a trail of blood as he tried to crawl away. The burning sensation traveling through his knee caps caused both of his legs to go completely numb. Real stood over top of him and let off another shot. BLOW! The hot slug pierced K.O.'s right elbow, shattering his cartilage into tiny pieces. Real's prey began screaming as he laid on his back and began urinating on himself.

Real wanted K.O. to know who was about to take his life and why, so he leaned down and grabbed him tightly by the shoulder. The black hoody made Real look like the grim reaper. He pointed his gun at K.O.'s head.

"I don't want your fucking crumbs nigga! I came for something else", Real growled. "Please! Just tell me what it is and I'll give it to you. I promise", K.O. pleaded.

K.O. tried to get a good look at Real's face but he didn't recognize him. A devilish grin appeared on Real's face as he removed the hood from his head. "My face look familiar to you?"

Real noticed the puzzled look on K.O.'s face.

"Remember 10 years ago, when that lady chased you up the hill with the ice pick?"

K.O.'s sudden change in his facial expression indicated that he remembered the incident very well.

"Yeah you remember that right! You remember me, the little boy that was standing right there when it happened?"

K.O. saw the crazed look in Real's blood shot eyes and knew he was about to die. He started shaking uncontrollably, completely lost for words. Real pulled out a long Rambo knife from the knife holster he kept on his belt buckle. He forcefully swung it, stabbing K.O. in the jugular vein in his neck. You could actually hear the sound of his adams apple pop as Real yanked the knife out. Thick globs of dark blood began squirting everywhere.

Real stood up and looked down at K.O.'s lifeless body laying sprawled out on the pavement. He walked away quickly from the gruesome scene with the bloody knife in on hand, and the hot gun in the other. A feeling of relief suddenly came over him.

CHAPTER 9

Peezo reached his hand in the backseat and grabbed a blue gym bag before getting out of his vehicle. He began surveying the area as he walked down the long dark street towards a large building. Once he made it to the front door, he walked straight inside to meet his connect.

The connect was standing near a long table on the left side of the dusty and gloomy looking warehouse. Tall piles of junk were everywhere.

"What it is J Black", Peezo greeted with a half smile.

He slapped hands with his supplier, and placed the gym bag on the table.

"What's going on man. You're two weeks late. Money must've slowed up on you huh?" J Black responded with a displeased face.

J Black, a dark skin short man, was a high ranking member of the notorious Black Gorilla Mob. Not only did they over populate and control the drug trade in the state of North Carolina, but they were also well known for deadly tactics when it came down to eliminating their competition.

Peezo breathed heavily out of his nose while looking away for a few seconds, knowing exactly why his paper flow slowed up. Real put his favorite *eliminate all the competition* tactic in to play by having J.J. and his team sell the coke pure for the cheapest price.

"Yeah man, money did slow up. I came across a little problem, but all of that shit is about to change tonight."
"I hope so", J-Black said with raised his eyebrows.

Peezo had been watching Real's house for some time now. He and two of his goons had plans on robbing Real for everything then killing him..

All of a sudden the loud sound of a gunshot echoed throughout the warehouse. BOOM! A . 357 slug chewed through the back of J Blacks head causing brain fragments to splatter all over Peezo's face and clothes. J Black slowly fell to the ground sideways, he died instantly.

Peezo was in complete shock. His wide eyes watched J Black's body jerk and shake. A thick puddle of blood began to form on the ground, outlining the slain man's body. When Peezo finally looked up he saw Wild Sal standing in front of him a few feet away with a blue steel . 357 aimed at his head. Wild Sal snuck through the back door of the warehouse, and crept up on the two men.

"See what you made me do", Wild Sal said with an evil grin on his face.

Scared to death, Peezo gasped for air.
"Oh shit man...oh...shit..what I do", he asked fumbling with his words.
"You turned down the proposition my nephew offered you", Wild Sal responded calmly.

"Awe man shit, I ain't no J.J. and them was gonna be on it like this. Please don't shoot me", Peezo begged, his voice began to crack. "So what you saying, you gonna start spending all ya money with my nephew if I let you live?"

Wild Sal fought to hold back his laugh, he got a kick out of niggas that bitched up right before they got their head blown off.
"Hell yeah man. I'll sell coke for them niggas for free!"

Peezo's eyes began to tear up. Wild Sal paused and thought about it for a minute. "Nah, too late."

Wild Sal squeezed the trigger. BOOM! The bullet hit Peezo in the forehead causing him to fall backwards on the ground. Wild Sal grabbed the bag of money and bag of drugs before disappearing behind the piles of junk that congested the warehouse.

The day Real sent J.J. to present the proposal to their competition he made Sal follow him.

for safety measures. That's when Sal noticed Peezo following J.J. He was going to murder him that same day, but Real told him to fall back. His plan was to have Sal follow Peezo's every move until he revealed his connect, and then murder them both. That's exactly what he did. After Peezo's demise J.J. and his crew took over his entire operation.

CHAPTER 10

There was a decent amount of people standing around in the projects. Snake Eyes and two of his loyal goons, Rocky and Nino, sat on the benches in front of Real's sister old building smoking a dutch of purple haze. Snake Eye's wasn't stupid or slow. Whenever he came to Real's old territory he made sure he came with two or more of his trusted shooters. They always packed heavy artillery just in case someone from the area grew enough courage to try and avenge Real's death. Even though they obediently submitted to his unexpected takeover, Snake Eyes knew deep down in their hearts they hated him with a passion.

"Damn man, where her sssexy asss at", Snake Eyes hissed anxiously.

His eyes were glued on the parking lot entrance while he waited on Dynasty's car to pull up. He called her 20 minutes before and told her to meet him in the projects.

"Big bro", Rocky said while handing Snake Eyes the dutch.
Snake Eyes took a pull of the haze and blew a thick cloud of smoke in the air. He turned to see one of his workers serving a fiend outside of the building and frowned.

"What the fuck thisss lil nigga doing. Here, take the weed."

After handing Nino the dutch, Snake Eyes stormed towards the young worker.
"Didn't I tell all you hard head asss niggasss to ssserve all the fiendsss insside the hallwaysss!"

He snatched the young boy up by his jacket, pulled out a black .44 magnum, and began pistol whipping him.

The worker began to yell as he tried desperately to block the violent blows that crashed against his head. People were looking out their windows and coming outside of their hallways to watch the violent scene. Snake Eyes quickly became tired and out of breath so he had to stop his brutality.

"Now go clean yassself up and get back to work!"

Snake Eyes released his grip from the bloody jacket. The young man was humiliated and afraid so he darted inside the building and did exactly what he was told. Snake Eyes turned around and realized everyone was looking at him.

"What the fuck everybody looking at!" He roared.

Rocky and Nino were laughing uncontrollably which caused him to chuckle to himself. He knew at that point he over did it again.

"I hope y'all ain't sssmoke all the haze", he said as he approached the bench to sit back down.

About twenty minutes had passed when a wide smile spread across Snake Eyes rough face. He was pleased to see Dynasty's car finally pulling inside the parking lot. She parked directly in front of the building across from where him and his crew sat.

Dynasty wore a black leather jacket and a pair of tight fitting blue jeans. She got out of her car and started walking towards Snake Eyes. *Damn why everybody looking at me all crazy,* she asked herself. Dynasty felt awkward when she noticed the majority of the people staring at her were real soldiers. They made sure to keep their mouths shut, but still shook their heads in disgust.

"What's up baby", Snake Eyes greeted smoothly with a slight grin on his face.

He stood up from the bench and gently wrapped his hand around her small waist, softly kissing her forehead. Snake Eyes got a kick out of the surprised and displeased looks on everyone's face when Dynasty pulled up. The only reason Snake Eyes told her to meet him in the projects was because he wanted it to be known that after murdering the king and conquering his castle, he also took his queen.

Oh my goodness, I know this dirt bag ain't just put his crusty ass lips on me. Dynasty was so disgusted but still managed to maintain her composure. She had already devised a strategic plan from beginning to end, but she forgot to prepare herself mentally for all the touching and smooching she would have to endure while in Snake Eyes' presence.

Dynasty moved her head back.
"Damn, we moving kind of fast ain't we. You kissing me in public and shit", she stated in a sweet tone trying not to sound angry.
"That's my fault. I couldn't help myself", he stated while licking his dark purple lips. Snake Eyes' lustful eyes slowly looked her up and down, from head to toe. Dynasty could see it all in Snake Eyes' face that he was head over heels for her. This of course gave her the upper hand as far as her plan was concerned, she just had to find out how far she could go.

Dynasty looked at the two young thugs sitting on the bench and said to Snake Eyes, "I know you ain't call me out here to chill up in the raggedy ass projects all day with you and your little flunkies while y'all hustle."

Rocky immediately twisted his face up. "Who the fuck..."

Before he could finish his sentence Snake Eyes quickly looked at him and gestured for him to stop.
"Fall back."

Rocky shut his mouth and stared at Dynasty with the evil eyes. *Who the fuck this bitch think she is. I'll blow her fucking head off,* Rocky thought to himself as he glanced at Nino. Dynasty began laughing to herself, still maintaining a straight face.

"Nah, we ain't gonna be up in thessse projectsss all day. I just had to pick up sssomething. That's why I told you to meet me up here. We can go do whatever you want, it's all up to you."

Dynasty stared into his eyes for several seconds trying to think of something to do.
"I want to go shopping."

"Say no more. Hold this shit down out here while I'm gone", he ordered before him and Dynasty went to his car.

Snake Eyes and Dynasty arrived at the Short Hills mall. Snake Eyes told Dynasty not to act shy and she was welcome to get whatever she wanted. This was definitely something he did not have to say twice. Dynasty shopped like a celebrity and spent hours going from store to store spending the enemy's money as if he had houses filled to the brim with money. She was throwing everything in the bag, so much that it took them 4 trips to the car to get all the bags in.

The expensive purchases weren't even for Dynasty, they were for Qadeesha. Dynasty told herself that she would make Snake Eyes pay dearly for beating her cousin the way he did. For now she was literally making him pay, but later she would make him suffer the severe punishment that awaited him.

Dynasty gasped and put her hands over her mouth. "Oh my gosh, look at this gorgeous bracelet", she said excitedly.

She stared in awe at the chunky bracelet flooded with VVS diamonds that glowed in the jewelry store display. The bracelet stood out from all the other jewelry that was placed around it.

"Which one, the big one in the middle?" Snake Eyes asked while standing beside her.

He liked the feeling of having her by his side. Some of the customers inside of the jewelry store stopped to stare at the couple. Dynasty smiled.

"Yup, that one."
"If you want it, get it."

Being the wifey to a man of Real's caliber, Snake Eyes knew Dynasty was well acquainted with the finer things. He told himself he was going to buy her whatever she wanted, just so he could prove that her baby dad was no where near his level.

One of the salesman spotted Dynasty and Snake Eyes looking as though they were interested in making a purchase. The light skin gay young man walked over to assist them.

"May I help you", he asked politely in a feminine tone.

Snake Eyes noticed the gay man and frowned in disgust. *Man look at this gay ass nigga*, he thought. Dynasty saw the look on Snake Eyes' face and began chuckling.

"Yes, I would like to try on that bracelet right there", she said pointing to the bracelet.

The salesman became excited at the chance to sale such a high priced item and rushed behind the counter to get the diamond bracelet. Dynasty put her arm out, allowing the him to put the bracelet on.

"Oh my goodness girl, this bracelet is a perfect match for you. It really looks amazing and it compliments your petite wrist."

The salesman began working his magic, making Dynasty feel pretty and Snake Eyes proud. Dynasty flicked her wrist back and forth causing the brilliant diamonds to sparkle.

"Girl let me hurry up and get behind you in case you faint after seeing the price tag", the salesman said jokingly but serious at the same time.

"Man the price don't matter. If that's what you want then get it babe."

The salesman could feel the vibe and immediately got quiet, not wanting to mess up his sale.

"Damn baby, chill out. He just joking."

Dynasty gently rubbed her soft hand on the side of Snake Eyes' face, causing him to blush. She then looked at the price tag.
"Baby this bracelet cost 50 grand."

The gay salesman put his hand on his hip, shifting his weight to the opposite side. *Um hum big baller, what ya skinny long neck ass got to say now*, he said to himself while starring at Snake Eyes waiting for his reaction.

"Like I said, if you want it get it."

Snake Eyes made sure to emphasize every word.

"Oh my goodness, thanks baby. If my baby dad was still alive he would have never bought me a bracelet this expensive."

Dynasty knew exactly what to say to stroke his ego. Snake Eyes paid for the bracelet with one of his credit cards, and he and Dynasty finally exited the mall.

On their way back to Trenton Snake Eyes asked Dynasty to stay the night with him, but she declined and told him she had to go home to her daughter. She also told him that she was going out of town to spend some time with her mother and would be back in a few weeks.

It was just getting dark when Dynasty finally pulled up to Qadeesha's house. She took her cell phone off the charger and texted her cousin to come outside to help with all the bags. Qadeesha wore a long blue robe when she came walking out the front door. Dynasty was so happy to see her cousin come outside. She unlocked the doors and popped the trunk.

"Oh so you snuck off and went shopping without out me huh", Qadeesha said.

She got a good look inside the back seat and noticed the pile of bags.
"Damn! Where you get the money to buy the whole mall?"

"I'ma tell you when we get in the house. It's more bags in the trunk."

After they carried all of the bags in the house, the two cousins sat down in the living room. Qadeesha was eager to find out who the mystery buyer was.

"So now tell me, who done took you out and bought you all this shit."

"This ain't my shit, most of the stuff in these shopping bags is for you."

A perplexed look appeared on Qadeesha's face. "What you mean most of this is mine?" "You heard what I said."

Dynasty paused long enough to keep her cousin in suspense.

"I had that same sucker ass nigga that you caught pissing on Kaze's grave take me out on the town and buy you all this expensive designer shit. Oh and look what else he bought you."

Dynasty pulled a black suede box from out of her jacket and opened it. Qadeesha's eyes lit up at the sight of the sparkling bracelet. Dynasty smirked at Qadeesha's face, feeling good for bringing some joy to her cousin. "Real bitches do real shit! Now take it and try it on. The only time I might have to wear it is when I go around that skinny snake looking piece of shit."

Once everything settled in, Qadeesha began to have mixed emotions and was lost for words. Before she could muster up the words to express how she felt, Dynasty kept going.

"He's infatuated with me, and will do whatever I say."

She grabbed her cousins hand and looked her deep in the eyes.

"Don't even trip, he's gonna get what he got coming to him. Trust and believe that", Dynasty assured with a devious look in her eyes. "But never mind all of that, let's see how you look in all this fly shit."

For the rest of the night Dynasty and Qadeesha laughed and joked, tried on the new designer clothes, and reminisced about the good times back when Kaze was alive.

CHAPTER 11

Qadeesha was feeling unhappy about Dynasty leaving and going back down south. Dynasty promised her that she would be back with Zanyah in a month, which helped to ease some of the sadness.

"Damn girl, I'm going to miss you", Qadeesha said as she hugged her cousin.
"I'm gonna miss you too. Don't worry, I'll be back before you know it", Dynasty stated trying to comfort Qadeesha.

Dynasty still wished she could take Qadeesha with her but she knew she had to respect her baby father's decision. BEEP! BEEP! A yellow taxi cab pulled up in front of Qadeesha's house.

"Alright, let me go before I miss my train."

Dynasty kissed her cousin on the cheek and rushed off to the front door.

During much of the long and boring train ride Dynasty pondered whether or not she should tell Real about the run-in she had with Snake Eyes. She couldn't come up with a decision, so she told herself she was going to keep everything in the dark until she figured out exactly what she was going to do.

Dynasty finally dozed off and slept a few hours, waking up 30 minutes before her stop. She texted Real to tell him to pick her up from the trains station. Dynasty exited the train station and began walking through the crowded parking lot where she spotted Real sitting on the hood of his car looking dead at her.

Real was smiling, holding a dozen of red roses in his hand. Dynasty's face turned red as she began to blush at the sight of her man. Real handed her the flowers and stuck his thick tongue down her throat as he gently grabbed the back of her neck. Their juicy wet full lips clamped together while their tongues played a passionate game of tug of war.

"Ummm", Dynasty moaned as her moist kitty cat began to purr. "Thank you baby, I missed you so much", she said in between kisses.

Her small hand firmly grabbed Real's rock hard penis. She stopped to stare at him with a naughty look in her eyes. Real knew exactly what she wanted. "Let's hurry up and head home so you can show me how much you miss me."

Real grabbed his lady by the hand and led her towards the car.

As soon as they walked through the front door Real and Dynasty began lip locking again, eagerly exploring each other's body. With his tongue still in Dynasty's mouth, Real used his foot to kick the door closed. He then scooped his love up in his strong arms and carried her up the stairs.

Real opened the master bedroom door and laid Dynasty down on their king size bed. Rose petals were placed all over the bed on top of the silk sheets. All of the lights were off, and candles were lit around the room creating a romantic glow. A bowl of crushed cherries were on the dresser near the bed. Dynasty and Real slipped out of their clothes.

"Lay on ya stomach", Real demanded.

Real grabbed the bowl of cherries and began to pour them down the center of Dynasty's back, all the way down to the cuff of her voluptuous ass. He then got on all fours over top of Dynasty and began licking the cherries from off her back. Dynasty started moaning as soon as she felt Real's warm tongue caressing her back.

Real sucked and licked greedily down the trail of cherries, leaving nothing behind.

"Oh daddy", she moaned out loud.

Dynasty arched her back as her spine shivered. She grabbed hold to the silk sheets as her juices began to pour down from her honey pot. Real licked her yellow fanny spotless and sat up on his knees.

"Turn over", he said in a low tone.

Dynasty rolled over to face her king and licked her lips at the sight of his big black 10 inch rod. "Daddy...I want it."

She cuffed one of her breast and began sucking on her pink erect nipple. Dynasty spread her thick legs wide and began rubbing her fingers on her swollen clitoris. Loud moans escaped her lips, echoing throughout the bedroom. The juices were still pouring from her slit, leaving a huge wet spot on the sheets. The light from the candles in the dark room made it appear as if Dynasty's rich yellow skin was glowing. Real just sat there and watched the show that the love of his life put on for him.

After a few minutes of play Dynasty was ready for her man.
"Lay down so I can take you on a long ride", she told Real.

Real snapped out of the trance he was in and laid back. Dynasty climbed on top of him and stuck her finger in his mouth, letting him taste her juices. The feeling of his warm tongue had her tempted to sit on his face, but instead she grabbed hold of his long pole and stuck it inside of her soaking wet pussy, slowly sliding down on it.

"Ummm", she moaned.

She pressed her hands down on his chiseled chest and threw her head back as she began grinding slowly back and forth, up and down. Real's body tensed up immediately. The pleasant feeling of Dynasty's tight wetness felt like he had just entered the pearly gates of heaven.

"You missed that dick didn't you?"

He cuffed her breast with one hand, and grabbed the back of her neck pulling her closer to him with his other hand. He began to suck on her erect nipple, twirling his tongue around and around. He was well aware of all the sensitive spots on Dynasty's body. He knew exactly what drove her wild, and this was one of them.

"Oooh yes...yes I miss my big black dick so much", Dynasty moaned as a tingling sensation traveled through her body.

She bit down on her bottom lip and began grinding faster and harder for a few minutes before Real took complete control of the situation. Real quickly wrapped his strong hands around Dynasty's slim waist and began pounding her guts in relentlessly. All you could hear was the sound of her gushy wet honey pot and their body's smacking against one another.

Real's long pole felt so good, Dynasty couldn't help but look down and watch him slide in and out of her. The way he manhandled her, and the sight of her sweet juices glistening on his six pack caused Dynasty to have back to back orgasms.

"Awe shit...yes...fuck me", she moaned out loud.

Her lips quivered and her eyes rolled to the back of her head as she grabbed hold of Reals chest, squeezing as tight as she could.

Dynasty's titties bounced around in Real's face, and he could actually see her big ol' yellow booty jiggling from the font as he continued to pound her. The light of the candles showed their shadows on the wall as they sexed each other like two wild beasts in the middle of the jungle.

The two went on and on and all you could hear was loud grunts and smell the sweet scent of sweaty sex in the air. Dynasty was now riding Real cowgirl style. Her soft booty jiggled all over the place as she continued to grind his manhood fiercely. She looked back at Real and the sexy facial expressions he made turned her on. It let her know she was doing the damn thing.

The silk sheets were soaked from their sweaty bodies. Dynasty was so out of control, bucking wildly, Real could do nothing but hold on tight to her small feet. He loved to watch her soft booty bounce all around his chocolate pole. SLAP! Real slapped her on the ass, leaving his hand print. A low scream escaped Dynasty's lips as a stinging sensation began throbbing on her left ass cheek. Turned all the way on, she began grinding so hard that Real's penis began to hurt. She leaned forward and grabbed hold to Real's ankles.

Real felt her body tense up and knew exactly what time it was.
"Ahh...I'm about...I'm about to...I'm cumming", she roared.

Dynasty looked down at her thick creamy juices pour down Real's shaft and balls as she shivered uncontrollably. The overflowing feeling of her warm wetness caused Real to explode also.

"Uggh!", he grunted out loud as his thick semen shot all the way up inside of her.

CHAPTER 12

Real, Wild Sal, and All Things were seated at a round table inside of a very expensive seafood restaurant several towns from where Real lived. They always met up with All Things in this restaurant whenever he came to visit. All Things made it his personal duty to come check up on his protege and his new investment at least once a month.

"We got this shit on smash. Every major trap star in the area get their work from us", Real stated proudly.

He took a sip of the champagne. All Things grinned while nodding his head up and down.
"I can tell, numbers never lie", he stated smoothly.

All Things knew that Real could conquer any town he chose to set up shop in, he just didn't think he would do it in such a short period of time. He was highly impressed.

"The next move is to spread out and take over town after town until we got the whole state under our control", Real explained.

The ambition in his voice was evident. Wild Sal looked at him while quietly eating a plate of shrimp. All Things began to think about what Real just proposed.

"Are you sure your soldiers are ready for that?"

All Things thought Real's purpose was to come down south for a short period of time, get his paper back up, and build a strong army so he could go back to Trenton and seek revenge; not conquer the whole state of North Carolina.

"Hell yeah, why wouldn't they be. My soldiers was born ready", Real responded. "Right, but I'm quite sure there's someone with a solid organization and a very strong hold on this state already. So if you plan on doing what you just explained, it means that you're going to be cutting into their pockets. Just make sure you're prepared for war once

y'all bump heads", All Things explained calmly.

Real already thought of that, but overlooked it. "Yeah I..."

Before Real could finish his sentence, he felt his cell phone vibrating.
"Oh shit, my phone. Yo", he answered.
"A yo big bruh, man these Black Gorilla Mob niggas out here talking 'bout they boss want to talk to you", J.J. said in a nervous tone. "The Black Gorilla Mob", Real repeated.

He frowned and glanced at All Things and Wild Sal. "How the fuck them niggas know who I am."

The name of the mob sounded familiar, but Real couldn't put a finger on who exactly they were and what they were about.

"I don't know man, but please just hurry up and come out here. I'm at the spot", J.J. pleaded.

"Alright man, I'm on my way now", Real assured before hanging up. "That was lil bro, he said some Black Gorilla Mob niggas out there talking about they boss want to talk to me. He sounded kinda' shook too. Let's hurry up and see what this shit is about."

Real stood up from his seat and hurriedly walked towards the exit door, All Things and Wild Sal followed behind him. Real and Wild Sal drove straight to J.J.'s trap spot while All Things went to the hotel he rented for the week.

As Real pulled up he surveyed the area and parked down the street from J.J.'s. He spotted two black tented out SUV trucks and J.J. standing on the porch along with 4 unfamiliar men dressed in all black. "There they go right there", Real said to Wild Sal.

Wild Sal sat in the passenger seat with both of his hands inside the side pockets of his long black trench coat. He was gripping two black twin .50 caliber Desert Eagles. The two men got out of the car and began walking towards the house.

When Real and Wild Sal stepped on the porch, one of the Black Gorilla Mob members was standing there. "My boss G-Black wants to have a few words with you", he said in a firm tone.

The BGM member stood two steps in front of three other men with his hands folded across his chest. Real glanced at J.J. who had an uneasy look on his face.

"If he just wanted to talk why does it take four of y'all to come and let me know?" "Because after hearing what's in the air we didn't know how you and ya crew was going to react when we approached you", he responded.

After hearing what's in the air? Real thought to himself. He began to wonder what the Black Gorilla Mob member was talking about. Without saying a word Real turned to look at

Sal who was standing close beside him, ready for whatever.

"Alright, take me to your boss", Real ordered.

Everyone walked off the porch and headed towards their vehicles. They finally pulled up in front of what looked like a bar or club. Real noticed a sign on the building wall that said: *GET DRUNK AND DO WHAT YOU WANT.*

Once parked, all the men got out of their cars and began walking through the gigantic parking lot towards the entrance door. The BGM members led the way while Real, Wild Sal, and J.J. followed. When they walked inside they saw an old brown skin man with grey dreadlocs wiping down the bar counter. "They in the back waiting", he said, barely looking up at them.

The men made it to the back where G-Black, a tall dark skin muscular man with long dreads, was seated with his feet kicked up on the table. He was talking to his underboss T-Dow, a light skin dread head. After hearing the door close, G-Black stopped talking and turned to

see is expected guest entering the room. He removed his feet from off the table and sat up in his chair.
"Everyone please be seated", G-Black grinned slyly.

"There's no need for us to get comfortable, we rather stand", Real said firmly making sure to look G-Black in the eyes.

Real stood on the opposite end of the long table, in the middle of Wild Sal and J.J. The light skin dread head frowned.
"Who the fuck..."

Before he could finish his sentence G-Black, who never broke his stare from Real, motioned his hand to silence hot headed T- Dow.

"Alright, if that's what y'all wanna do so be it."

G-Black was trying to remain calm, but he was getting frustrated. The negative energy began traveling throughout the room as everyone stared at each other for a few seconds.

"My reason for wanting to speak with you is because one of my most honorable men and one of his biggest spenders were robbed and murdered in the middle of a transaction that took place in the same town you just so happened to pop up in. So I figured out of all people you would be able to help me find out who did it. Here's a picture of them."

G-Black handed them to one of his soldiers to hand to Real to look at. He was trying to read Real's body language.

Who the fuck this nigga think I am, Real thought to himself. He had a funny feeling that he knew exactly who G-Black was talking about. The henchman approached Real and handed him the picture. *I knew it man damn! What the fuck was I thinking,* Real thought. After seeing the picture of Peezo Real pretty much figured out how his identity was exposed and kicked himself in the ass for not having Wild Sal kill him the same night he followed J.J. to his house.

Real stared at the picture for a few seconds before showing Wild Sal and J.J.
"Do any of these faces look familiar to y'all", he asked.

J.J. and Wild Sal both shook their heads and said "nah" at the same time. Real went over to G-Black and placed the pictures in front of him on the table. "Nah bruh, we don't know those niggas", Real said plainly.

"Oh yeah. Y'all don't know nothing about nothing huh", T-Dow stated sarcastically shooting Real the twenty five to life.

Without saying a word, Real shot T-Dow an ill look and then focused his attention back on G-Black.

"I kind of figured that y'all wouldn't know anything. Anyway, I came up with a proposition for you."

This black ugly muhfucka can't be serious, Real said to himself as he smirked. "Oh yeah, and what would that be", he asked trying to sound interested.

"Spend your money with me and my family and we will front you however many bricks you buy and continue to allow you to spread your horizons in our state."

"What's the price on a key", Real asked. "Twenty seven."

Real kept a straight face while staring at G- Black, but inwardly he wanted to burst into laughter. He found it comical that G-Black was trying to offer him a price higher than he was already getting it for. Not to mention the coke that Wild Sal robbed and killed his soldier for was stepped on at least three times. "Let me get a sample."

G-Black turned to his underboss. "T-Dow, you got some on you right?"

T-Dow pulled out a hundred gram pack and placed it on the table.

"Give me your cell number and I'll holla at you in two to three weeks at the most to let you know what it is", Real said before picking up the plastic bag of coke.

Real and his crew exited the bar. G-Black and his crew watched them leave. While they were walking back to the car J.J. wanted to know where Real's head was at. "You really going to fuck with them Black Gorilla Mob niggas on the coke tip?"

"Hell no! I just told that funny looking ass nigga that. If I would've said no they probably would have killed us inside. The time I told him to give me is just enough time for me to find out everything about their leader and kill them before the war they trying to make even start."

Wild Sal, who loved war with a passion, burst into a loud laughter as all three of them got inside the car. He was looking forward to the drama.

CHAPTER 13

Real found out all the information he needed to know about G-Black and his underboss T- Dow and planned to assassinate them after dark tonight. Real wasn't sure how things would turn out after the two were murdered, so he packed up his family's belongings to move to another town once the hit was done. The only reason he didn't move his family before the hit was because it would have ruined Za-Za's first birthday party that was also taking place today.

It was a nice sunny day outside, around 80 degrees. Different members of the family from both sides and friends from the neighborhood were enjoying themselves in the front and back yard. Some of them were playing cards, some sat in chairs listening and bobbing their heads to the music, while others spent their time drinking telling jokes and laughing with each other. There were also some that just stood around watching how the crowd of little kids reacted to the clown show.

Dynasty was cooking on the grill fixing plates while Real was video recording Za-Za who was being held by his older sister Tadasia. Zanyah wore a pink and white Prada dress with Prada sandals to match. Real did everything he possibly could to make sure his baby girl had an unforgettable first birthday.

"Smile Za-Za", Tadasia said.

Tadasia was the only one who knew that her brother faked his death back in Trenton, so whenever she came to visit she made sure to come by herself.

"Smile for the camera little mama", Real cheered as he zoomed in on his daughter's pretty little face.

He reached his hand out and tickled her on her belly, getting her excited. Zanyah's face lit up whenever she interacted with her daddy, she had a whole lot to say.

Kim waited impatiently for Dynasty to fix her plate as she sat at one of the tables with a few of her friends. They were playing a card game called Pitty Pat, gambling for money.
"Damn Dynasty, what's taking ya ol' yellow self so long with my plate."

Kim spoke loud enough to be heard over the music. Dynasty mumbled in frustration. "Here I come mom."

She carefully walked towards her mother with two plates filled with food in her hand. Dynasty been in the country long enough to pick up the accent.

"Kim honey it's your turn to pluck a card out the deck", Kim's friend Nicky said.

Kim refocused back on the game. She reached to grab the top card from the deck. Kim smirked when she saw the number 2 card in her hand.

"Pitty Pat!" she exclaimed excitedly chuckling.

Kim slammed the cards on the table revealing three deuces and grabbed the winnings out of

the basket that sat in the center of the table. Everyone else threw their hands in and began sipping on their Corona's. Dynasty approached the table.

"Here mom, here Nicky."

Dynasty placed both of the paper plates on the table.

"Thank you honey", Nicky said before she sat her beer on the table and grabbed her plate of food. "You're welcome."
Dynasty looked across the yard and noticed the clowns entertaining the crowd of children, but didn't see

Zanyah. *What the fuck they think this is*, she said to herself. She began walking towards the clowns. "What the hell y'all all the way over here for?"

The colorful clowns stopped immediately to look at Dynasty standing there with her hands on her hips. "My baby dad ain't pay y'all to just entertain these lil kids. Y'all better go over there and entertain my daughter too. She the birthday girl."

The clowns began walking towards Real, Zanyah, and Tadasia. J.J. and his girlfriend Nu-Nu were standing a few feet away leaning on the hood of a car smoking a blunt. They burst into laughter at how Dynasty just blacked out on the clowns. Dynasty turned to see who was laughing.

"What so funny?"
"Ya crazy ass", J.J. responded in between laughs holding the blunt in his hand.
"Ain't nobody crazy, they better go do what they asses got paid to do. But anyway, can you run to mommy house real quick and grab some more hot dogs, burgers, and sodas from out the fridge lil bro?"
J.J. let out a deep breath. He was high out of his mind and was enjoying the wonderful scenery, the last thing he felt like doing was running an errand. "Alright man, damn."

J.J. was on his way down the street to his moms house when Dynasty yelled out at him again.
"Hold up, you gonna need some help. Where the hell Uncle Sal at?"

Her green eyes scanned the front yard.

"There he go right there", J.J. yelled, spotting Sal across the street standing against a tree watching everyone enjoying themselves.

Dynasty began waving her hand for him to come towards her.

"Uncle Sal, come here. I need you to do something for me."

She could tell that he didn't hear her over the loud music, so she shouted even louder. "Uncle Sal come here!"

Sal heard his name and began walking towards Dynasty.
"What's up?", he said.

Wild Sal became really tight with everybody during the time they spent together, and was now considered family.

"Uncle Sal, can you please walk down the street to my mom house with my brother and help him carry back some food and drinks for the party", Dynasty asked in an innocent tone. "Yeah, I got you."

Sal looked at J.J. "Come on", he said.

Nunu was left there holding the blunt.

"Girl you mine as well put that out and come over here and enjoy the party", Dynasty said.

Real was laughing as he recorded everything on the camera. The look on his daughters face was all he needed to make him happy. She was still being held in her aunts arms watching the group of colorful clowns do funny dances and tricks to entertain her. "You like the clowns huh Za-Za?" Tadasia said as she lowered her head to look in her niece's face.

A few other friends and family members including Dynasty watched from a few feet away in a small crowd. *My baby looking like what the hell*, Dynasty thought to herself smiling. She looked down the street and saw J.J. and Wild Sal walking from her mother's house carrying bags.

Suddenly, out of no where, a dark blue Benz pulled up in front of the house. A masked man holding a black Mac 11 machine gun quickly popped out the sun roof and began letting loose. RAT! TAT! TAT! TAT! TAT! TAT! TAT!

Everyone was screaming and hollering, scared for their lives. People were scattering like roaches and ducking for cover as a gang of bullets flew indiscriminately through the crowd. Slugs ripped through the three clowns and a few other people standing near them. Brains and blood splattered all over Zanyah and Tadasia. Real quickly dropped his camera and dove over top of them, using his body as a shield.

In one swift motion Dynasty dove on the ground and grabbed her black baby 9MM from off her hip. POP! POP! POP! POP! POP!

Dynasty began busting back at the masked man from her position laid out on the grass. She missed several shots but one of the slugs hit him dead in the throat. The man dropped his gun and began to moan in pain. His thick crimson red blood began leaking out like a faucet as he quickly wrapped his hand around his throat. The driver sped off recklessly down the street, causing the tires to screech.

By that time Wild Sal and J.J. dropped the bags and pulled out their pistols. The both of them started busting at the car as it sped towards them. BOOM! BOOM! BOOM! BOOM! BOOM! BOOM! BOOM! The bullets riddled the car as it flew past them. One of them went through the driver's window and pierced the side of the driver's head causing him to loose control of the steering wheel and violently crash into a house on the corner.

By the end of the shoot out all three of the clowns were dead, Dynasty's mother Kim was shot in the arm, and a few other family and friends also got hit. This was a clear statement

from the Black Gorilla Mob. The war was officially on!

G-Black knew damn well it didn't take two to three weeks to sell the little coke sample he gave Real. He tried to give the young boss the benefit of the doubt, but told himself that he would only wait two weeks. When he didn't receive a response, G-Black sent his soldiers to handle their handle.

CHAPTER 14

With the deadly war breaking out Real sent his family back to Trenton until everything was over. As soon as Dynasty stepped foot back in the city she spent every day with her prey, Snake Eyes. In a short period of time she learned his daily routines, had access to all of his money, and basically knew everything there was to know about his empire. Dynasty was playing her role to the fullest and had Snake Eyes' silly ass convinced that she belonged to him and nothing, nor no one would ever be able to come in between that. The funny thing about it all was that he didn't even get a chance to smell her panties yet. She told him he had to wait six months to a year to see what she tasted and felt like. Snake Eyes was more than willing to wait.

Usually Snake Eyes and Low Down rode around to collect and bring the money to Dynasty to put it in the safe house, but the two of them went up top to purchase more cocaine and heroin on this particular day.

"Damn man, where the hell the house at", Dynasty said. She squinted her eyes to try to see the numbers on the houses as she slowly drove down the dirty congested block of Locust St.

"Oh shit, here it is."

Dynasty pulled up in front of the house Snake Eyes told her to go and parked. She walked on the porch and began knocking on the door. Within seconds, a raspy voice spoke from behind the door.

"Who is it?" "It's Dynasty."

Rocky immediately opened the door. "Come in."

Ever since the day Dynasty tried to play Rocky he didn't like her, and she knew it by the ill vibe that shot off of his body whenever she came around.

Dynasty stepped inside and shut the door behind her. Rocky walked over to the blue couch and grabbed a black gym bag.

"Money was slow as hell the last two days. I'll have the other 15 grand tomorrow, it's 10 inside the bag", Rocky explained, trying to hand her the money.

Dynasty twisted her face up.
"What the fuck you mean you ain't got all the money. I know how this shit go. Let me find out ya lil flunky ass flipping my baby money." "Who the fuck you think you talking to! You better watch ya mouth!" Rocky said trying his best to keep his cool.

Hearing all the commotion, Nino walked from out the kitchen.
"What's going on?" Nino asked, but was ignored. "No nigga, who the fuck you think you talking to? You know what, I got something for ya ass."

Dynasty pulled her cell phone out and began dialing Snake Eyes cell number.

"I don't give a fuck if you call that nigga."

Rocky and majority of the members of their organization didn't respect how their boss let his feisty new found wifey be all up in the middle of their street business. Everyone was getting extremely fed up with Snake Eyes' recklessness. Dynasty knew it too and played on it every chance she got.

"What'sss up my love", Snake Eyes answered. "What's up baby. I came to lil Rocky spot to pick up what you told me to get but he said he was short..."

Before she could finish her sentence Snake Eyes said, "Oh don't worry about it."

"No but listen, after he told me he was short I told him he better not be trying no funny shit. Then he got all up in my face talking slick to me, raising his voice. Then when I started dialing your number he gon' yell at me talking bout he don't give a fuck."

"What! Put that lil nigga on the phone", Snakes Eyes yelled.

Dynasty handed Rocky the phone. Rocky started shaking his head.

"This sucker for love ass nigga", he mumbled under his breath.

"What you just say nigga? Speak up, you a gangsta right?" Dynasty taunted.

A sly smirk came across her face as she listened to Snake Eyes scream through the phone on his soldier. Dynasty knew exactly what she was doing. Every chance she got and in anyway she could she cunningly did things out of spite to make Snake Eyes abuse his authority on the men in his elite circle. She knew that would arouse resentment towards him and weaken the foundation of his empire. You have to admit, her baby dad taught her very well.

After Snake Eyes blacked out on Rocky, Dynasty grabbed her cell phone and the bag of money and went on her way.

Real's drug organization went head to head with the BGM. Their *wild wild west* gun battles moved from town to town. Real and Wild Sal were both out lurking trying to catch G-Black and T-Dow slipping, which seemed like the hardest thing in the world to do. They went to every single spot their sources told them, but the information always proved to be inaccurate. It was like they disappeared from the face of the earth. It was so bad that Wild Sal started to get extremely frustrated.

"Where the fuck these bitch ass niggas at", Sal grumbled in a low tone.

He was pacing back and forth inside the Holiday Inn hotel room. Sal had his dingy looking dread wig tied in a long pony tail and wore an all black army suit with matching gloves. Real was just as mad, but he still managed to keep his composure. He sat on the edge of the bed facing the wall, trying to come up with a solution on how they were going to go about finding their marks.

The BGM had showed their carelessness and disrespect in the highest order by shooting up Real's daughter's birthday party. The thought of Zanyah getting hit by a stray bullet caused his heart to burn deeply with rage. He wanted to murder G-Black and T-Dow so bad that every time he closed is eyes he saw them both sprawled out on the ground dead with gunshot wounds to the head. Real looked at Sal who was still pacing the floor.
"Big unc, calm down. We gonna find them niggas, we just gotta be patient."

"How the hell we gonna find 'em when we keep getting false information about they whereabouts. Them unreliable ass sources probably setting us the fuck up! We should start busting their asses too!"

Without saying a word Real just sat there watching Sal continuously pace the floor. He began brainstorming again on how he was going to find his enemies. Then if finally clicked - All Things! With his connections he could damn near find out whatever he wanted to know in America.

"Oh shit big unc! We can get All Things to find out where them niggas hiding at."

"Fuck All Things, he the one that killed ya pops."

Wild Sal immediately stopped in his tracks and looked Real dead in the face. He grew extremely attached to Real and his family and was tired of seeing All Things play the role of a father figure and mentor to Real when in actuality he was the true reason Real never had a chance to meet his dad. Not to mention, for many many years he hated the way All Things spoon fed him, talked to him any kind of way, and treated him like nothing more than a worthless servant. Sal told himself that all the bullshit was going to stop today and he meant it.

Real couldn't believe the words that just came out of Sal's mouth.

"What?" Real had to make sure he heard things correctly.

Sal breathed heavily out of his nose and lowered his head. He took a few steps forward and placed both hands on Real's shoulders.

"I'm tired of All Things' fake slime ball shit! He's the one who murdered ya pops back in the day", Sal emphasized every word.

Seeing the seriousness in Sal's face, Real squinted his eyes as his blood began to boil causing his heart rate to increase.

"Man get the fuck off me!" Real demanded, forcefully removing Sal's large hands from off his shoulders.

Real quickly stood up. Sal immediately took a few steps back, not knowing what to expect.

"How the fuck you know?" Real asked.

Sal glanced down at the floor and started shaking his head as his mind flashed back to the day he witnessed

Young A, now known as All Things, kill Big Real in that alleyway years ago.

"Because I was right there when he did it."

Real sighed out loud as a swarm of mixed emotions came over him. He flopped back down on the edge of the bed and slowly rubbed both of his hands across his face, blinking his eyes repeatedly. Real was taken all the way back. *Awe man, what the fuck. This shit can't be true,* he said to himself as his mind raced all over the place.

"I was gonna tell you as soon as you bailed out of jail but too much shit started happening at once. So I said I was gonna wait until everything cooled down before I put you up on that nigga", Wild Sal explained.

Real remained quiet for a moment. "Why did he do it?"

I'm going to have to sit down for this one, Sal thought to himself.
"All Things shot ya pops because he punched him in the mouth for not posting his bail when he was supposed to so he could be there when your mother gave birth to you."

Sal paused for a few seconds waiting for Real to respond but he didn't, so he continued.
"It was crazy because they were best friends. All Things claims that he didn't mean to kill him and he did it off of a quick reaction after being punched off guard. I guess guilt consumed him after that because he moved to Delaware and bought me with him and gave me whatever I wanted. The only reason he did that was because I was the only one that knew what really went down. I guess the nigga thought I was gonna tell on him or some shit. Even though I was smoking crack around the time, I still lived by the rules of the game. I would

have never went out like that, but I was smart and took advantage of the situation."

Real turned to face Sal.

"So you mean to tell me that my dad was murdered on behalf of me?"

The pain and anger was evident in Real's tone. He was a son of a man he never knew and that very fact penetrated his heart. Real grew up thinking his dad really didn't give two fucks about him, but come to find out the unconditional love his dad had for him was the cause of his demise.

"Yeah, that's what I'm telling you nephew."

Sal tried to console Real again and rested his hand on his shoulders.

"I told you the first time don't touch me you slime ball ass nigga!" He yelled.

Real stood up over top of Sal.

"Get the fuck out! Matter fact, you know what..."

Real grabbed the car keys off the dresser and stormed out of the hotel room, slamming the door behind him. After Real exited the hotel, he stormed through the parking lot, climbed inside his car and sped off recklessly.

Low Down and Snake Eyes made it back to Trenton safely with the work. They dropped everything off at their stash house and went straight to Rocky's spot. Low Down knocked on the door while Snake Eyes stood silently beside him.

"Who is it?" Rocky yelled. "It's me man, open the door."

Recognizing the voice, Rocky immediately took the locks off the door. As soon as Rocky opened the door Snake Eyes threw a leaping right hook that crashed against the side of Rocky's jaw. Rocky was caught off guard so he stumbled back and struggled to catch his balance, eventually falling to the ground.

"You disssressspected my lady lil nigga", Snake Eyes growled with clenched teeth as he rushed over top of him and began stomping him with his hard Gortex boots.

"Man she lying", Rocky tried to get a word in.

He quickly balled up on the floor, trying his best to block his face.
"I ain't disrespect her, she disrespected me!" "I don't want to hear that ssshit."

Snake Eyes continued to stomp Rocky out relentlessly. His boot prints started to show on Rocky's black hoody. Low Down shook his head as he watched his right hand man stomp out one of his most loyal soldiers down to the ground as if he was a complete stranger. *This bitch got this nigga going crazy*, Low Down thought to himself. He started feeling sorry for the little homie. Snake Eyes had already blacked out on Rocky for staring at Dynasty too long a few days ago.

"Alright man that's enough damn!" Low Down stated with his raspy voice.

He rushed to Rocky's aid and pulled Snake Eyes from off of him.
"You on some bullshit man, calm down."

Low Down knew he was going to rough Rocky up a little bit, but he didn't expect him to beat him senseless.

"Nah fuck that, thessse lil niggasss need to watch how they talk to people!"

Snake Eyes was still breathing heavily and trying to break loose from Low Down's grasp. The only reason

Snake Eyes didn't murder Rocky for disrespecting Dynasty was because he proved his loyalty several times and he was the only one that knew how to run all of his blocks the proper way. Rocky groaned out loud in pain, placing his hand on his rib cage where the excruciating pain throbbed. He slowly rolled over on his back looking up at the ceiling.

"I think...I...I think my shit broke", he gasped for air, struggling with his words.

Young Rocky loved Snake Eyes as if he was his big brother, but after being stomped to the ground like a worthless bum that got caught stealing, he immediately felt the total opposite. *I'm gonna murder this nigga! Fuck that! I put that on my life! Him and that scandalous ass bitch of his"*, he thought to himself. Rocky glanced over at Snake Eyes who had his cell phone out.

"Yo baby hurry up and come get me. I'm at Rocky ssspot."
"Alright honey, I'm on my way right now", Dynasty assured on the other end of the phone.

While Snake Eyes waited on Dynasty, Low Down took young Rocky to the hospital.

Later on that night, Snake Eyes and Dynasty were chilling at a 5 star hotel inside a jacuzzi watching *Paid in Full* on the gigantic flat screen that hung on the wall. The two of them were sipping on clear glasses of champagne. All of the lights were off, which gave the room a dim glow from the television screen.

"Damn baby, you could move a little clossser. I ain't gonna bite unlesss you tell me to", Snake Eyes said charmingly.
He reached his hand in the water and began rubbing on her thick thigh. *Oh my gosh! If this dirty ass nigga don't*

take his filthy hands from off me, Dynasty thought to herself in disgust. Her body immediately tensed up from Snake Eyes' creepy touch. She let out a fake laugh, taking her eyes off the T.V. to look into Snake Eyes' skinny rough looking face. *This nigga look sick,* she thought.

Snake Eyes' face was sunken in, causing every part of his bone structure to visibly show. It's sad to say, but the deadly virus definitely began taking it's tole on his body, especially since he didn't take the medicine the doctor prescribed. Snake Eyes was not taking care of himself properly.

"Damn baby, you alright?" He asked, feeling her body jump.
"Yeah, I'm good baby. You just touched my spot, that's all", she lied.

A seductive smile was on her beautiful face as she moved closer, brushing up against him. Snake Eyes' manhood became rock hard. "Yeah, that's more like it."

He gently placed his arm across her shoulder, and took a sip of the champagne. The both of them tried to focus back on the movie.

After being in the jacuzzi for almost an hour, Snake Eyes tried to talk Dynasty into letting him slide inside of her. He felt as though he put in more than enough work and deserved some pussy. Even though Dynasty wasn't trying to hear it, Snake Eyes already had it in his mind that as soon as she went into a deep sleep he was going to pull her panties to the side and slide his poisonous snake inside her fresh garden anyway. *Once she feel me inside her she gonna want to keep going,* Snake Eyes said to himself.

Snake Eyes' daydream was interrupted by the cell phone ringing on the dresser.
"Baby, can you grab my cell phone for me?"

Dynasty climbed out of the jacuzzi and began walking towards the dresser. She wore a hot pink two piece bikini. Snake Eyes lustful eyes were glued on her big round yellow ass as it jiggled with every step she took. Dynasty made her way back over to Snake Eyes with his phone.

"Here baby", she said softly.
"Hello."
"You dirty dick muthafucka! You gave me AIDS! I'm..."

Before the female on the other end could finish her sentence, Snake Eyes hung up and then looked at Dynasty.
"I ain't fronting that nigga no work, and I'm tired of him keep calling and asking", he said trying to play it off.

Different females that he hit always called him months later crying and cursing him out, so it really wasn't nothing new to him. Dynasty looked down at the phone and noticed it was blinking on and off again.

"Whoever it is, is calling you back."

Snake Eyes twisted his face up.
"Man this bitch ass nigga better leave me the hell alone."

Snake Eyes climbed out of the jacuzzi and went over to the bed and picked up his towel to dry off. All he wore was a black pair of silk boxers.

"I'm getting tired", Dynasty said as she yawned, putting her hand over her mouth.

She got out too and grabbed her towel to dry off.

Dynasty climbed in the bed and got under the sheets. Snake Eyes sat on the opposite side of the bed. He was rolling up some weed so he had his back turned to her. Dynasty stared at Snake Eyes' boney body frame and frowned her face in disgust. She never cheated on Real since the day she lost her virginity to him, and felt extremely out of pocket as she laid up in the bed undressed with Snake Eyes. She told herself she had to play her role to the fullest in order for things to go as planned.

"Oh my gosh, you about to smoke that stank shit. Damn!"

Dynasty hated the smell of weed smoke so she pulled the covers over her head and fell asleep. About forty-five minutes passed by, and Snake Eyes was high as a kite. He finally finished smoking and was getting under the covers to lay close beside Dynasty. He noticed her cell phone vibrating on the dresser so he grabbed it. When he looked at who was calling he saw DADDY on the screen. *Who the fuck is this?* He said to himself as he began to get angry.

Unbeknownst to him it was Real on the other end calling to check up on Dynasty and his daughter. Dynasty told Real to check in every couple of days, just so she can know he was alright. Snake Eyes answered the call.
"Who the hell is this", he asked in a low, but hostile tone.

He didn't here anyone respond so he asked again. "Yo man, who is this?"

He waited for a few seconds but still no response. He pulled the phone from his hear to look at it, and noticed the screen was blank because the battery went dead. "I'll find out who that was later on, but right now it's time to do what it do", he said to himself.

Dynasty's ass was poking out towards Snake Eyes as she lay on her side.

"Oh yeah, easy access", he said.

He stuck his head under the sheets, slipped out of his boxers and began stroking his penis. He then used his index finger to move her panties to the side in an attempt to slide the head of his erect penis inside of her slit. Dynasty quickly turned around and snatched the covers from off of him.

"Boy what the hell is you doing!"

Snake Eyes was stuck and lost for words as he lay there with his penis in his hand.

"What it look like? Ssshit, you gotta nigga waiting all long to ssse what that pusssy feel like. What you expect!"

Dynasty frowned.

"Oh yeah, well now ya ass gonna have to wait another six months!"

Snake Eyes sighed out loud as a feeling of anger and embarrassment came over him.

"So who the hell you got stored in your phone as Daddy?" He said trying to change the subject.

"Why the hell were you searching through my phone while I was sleep?"

Dynasty quickly sat up in the bed and looked at her phone on the dresser. The thought of Snake Eyes calling Real and finding out he was alive caused her chest to tighten and her heart to skip a beat. She knew he didn't

because he wouldn't have been questioning her about who it was.

"I wasssn't sssearching through your phone it started ringing, and when I went to anssswer it the battery went dead", Snake Eyes responded, sitting up in the bed. "Ssso who was it?"

"Exactly what it said nigga, my dad!" She responded moving her neck from side to side. "You never told me that you be ssstaying in contact with your dad. All you ever talk about is ya mom", he said looking at Dynasty suspiciously.

"That's because you never asked. Plus I don't like talking about my dad like that because he did a whole lot of bullshit when I was younger."

Dynasty could sense Snake Eyes' suspicion. "What, you don't believe me?"
"Nah it ain't like that. I just wanted to know who it wasss. But anyway, I ain't waiting no 6 more months to get sssome."

"Oh yes you is nigga", she said before getting out of the bed and walking towards the bathroom.

Oh my gosh he was really about to try and slide his dirty little dick inside me while I was sleep, she thought. Dynasty was so grateful that she woke up in time.

CHAPTER 15

Real cruised from town to town as his heart and mind did summersaults. Several days had passed since Wild Sal broke the news about his father's death. Real still couldn't get over the fact that the man he grew to love strongly over the years, as if he was his own pops, was responsible for the bullet that murdered his real dad. While growing up he heard a few stories about his father's demise, but now he finally knew what really went down. Every time he thought about it hot tears burned his eyes as the feeling of revenge caught him in his heart.

Even though Real never knew his dad, he felt more than obligated to make sure the sneaky motherfucker that murdered him laid 6 feet deep. The only unanswerable question that traveled through his mind was how would he do it without loosing his own life. All Things had the most powerful and secretive organization in the entire tri-state, so the feat seemed almost impossible. Not to mention, the uncooked beef he had with his worse enemy, Snake Eyes. Overall, he was in two very tough situations, and for the first time in a very long time he wasn't too sure as to how he would go about solving them.

"Oh shit!", Real exclaimed.

He slammed his black Gortex boots on the brake, and quickly reversed back behind the red light to avoid being hit by the blue pick- up truck speeding towards him. BEEP! BEEP! BEEP! BEEP!

"Get out of the middle of the road asshole!" The fat blonde hair white driver yelled at Real.

The man just missed the front of Reals car by a few inches. Real was so lost in deep thought, he stopped paying attention to the road. He also didn't notice the dark green tented out Chrysler that was following him ever since he left the hotel.

It was the BGM underboss T-Dow! Coincidentally, he and Real rented rooms at the same hotel. When T-Dow was walking out of his room, he spotted Real getting inside of his car and immediately went to follow him. T-Dow looked at the text message that just came in on his phone. It read: YOU AIN'T LOOSE THAT NIGGA DID YOU?

The message was from G-Black. T-Dow shook his head and texted back. NO. BUT IF YOU KEEP TEXTING ME EVERY 15 MINUTES I'LL FUCK AROUND AND LOOSE HIM. HIT ME UP IN A HOUR. EVERYTHING WILL BE TAKEN CARE OF.

Just as hard as it was for Real to find them, it was the same scenario on their side. So when T-Dow alerted G-Black that he had the drop on the enemy, he was very eager to get the war done and over with. That way they could get back to handling business.

The red light finally turned green, and Real slowly pulled off. *Damn man, I need to take my ass back to the room and get my thoughts together before I end up killing myself,* Real thought as he made his way back to the hotel. Real had to piss very badly, and new he wouldn't make it to the room in time, so he pulled over on a small side street before getting back on the highway.

One side of the street had a few houses, while the other side had nothing but tall oak trees. There was also a wooden bridge over top of a small lake that led to the other side of the field.

"Damn man I gotta piss bad as hell."

Real quickly parked his car and rushed to the field holding his crotch. He made sure he ran deep in the woods so no one in the houses could see him. Real made it behind one of the tall oak trees and began to relieve himself. "Fuck", he sighed, holding his head back.

While Real was taking a piss, T-Dow managed to quietly creep behind a tall tree that was about 10 feet away. He had his chrome 44 magnum in his hand.

Real finally finished and began walking back towards his car. T-Dow crept around the tree, precisely timing Real's every step. He was so eager to blow Real's brain out the front of his head his palms began sweating and his heart rate was at full speed. *This ol' city boy sweet like pussy*, T-Dow said to himself. He continued to slowly follow behind Real with his gun drawn. T-Dow was about 15 feet away, all he wanted to do was get a few feet closer so he could get a clean shot of the back of Real's head.

Suddenly, T-Dow clumsily stepped on a stick that was laying on the ground. Real heard the noise and immediately made an attempt to grab his gun from off his hip. BOOM! Real spun around and looked at T-Dow. His chest was wide open, the 12 gage slug that ripped through his heart caused him to die instantly. Wild Sal was standing a few feet away with an all black Moxberg shotgun in his hand. Thick gun smoke was still coming out of the huge barrel.

Not knowing what to say Real shook his head from side to side. Just a few minutes ago he was extremely angry with Wild Sal and didn't want him around, but now he was happy as hell to see him. Real knew that he had been caught slipping and would probably be dead right now if it wasn't for Sal. *Damn man, that was a close one foreal*, Real thought to himself.

Sal just stood there quietly, staring Real in the eyes and could tell everything that was going on in his mind.
"So what are we going to do just stand here and stare at each other until the cops come, or are we gonna finish handling our handle", Sal said seriously in a deep tone.

Before Real could utter a word, the loud sound of T-Dow's cell phone began ringing. Real kneeled down and rolled the heavy dead body over, and dug inside his pocket to get the phone. It was another text message from G-Black. YOU MEAN TO TELL ME YOU STILL AIN'T HANDLE THAT SWEET ASS CITY BOY YET?

Sweet city boy huh. I got something for ya black gorilla looking ass, Real thought to himself as he texted back. MEET ME IN FAYETTEVILLE ON BOND STREET IN FRONT OF THE RED BRICK HOUSE NEAR THE CORNER. G- Black quickly responded: I'M ON MY WAY RIGHT NOW. GIVE ME ABOUT 45 MINUTES. Real took T-Dow's car keys from out of his pants and tossed them to Sal.

"Drive the car."

G-Black was dressed in a dark green army fatigue jacket and had his long dreads in a french braid that hung down his back. He drove through slowly down Bond street in a black van until he finally spotted T-Dow's car lights blink on and off.

"There go my nigga right there", G-Black said with a huge smirk on his face.

He parked his car and got out, making his way to his comrade's car. G-Black began walking down the street, he kept his hand tucked in his jacket pocket tightly gripping on a black .40 caliber handgun. All of a sudden he heard Phantom's lyrics loudly playing through the speakers of T-Dow's car. G-Black knew one of the back windows had to be down because of the way the extremely loud music echoed through the entire block.

Real was hiding on the side of a house waiting for his prey. As soon as G-Black passed, Real crept up with the 12 gauge drawn to the back of G-Black's head. BOOM! Without giving G-Black the privilege of seeing who was sending him to meet his maker, Real sent the huge bullet crashing through his skull, causing his brains to splatter all over the place. There was nothing left but his chin and the bottom of his mouth as G-Black's lifeless body stiffened up before falling sideways to the ground.

CHAPTER 16

After destroying the head and tail of the Black Gorilla Mob, the entire body of the organization crumbled completely. This left Real and his empire with supreme control over the drug trade in the huge state of North Carolina. As time passed, Real's empire grew tremendously, overpopulating majority of the towns in the state thanks to J.J. and his crew. Real was able to stack his paper up to the clouds, accomplishing millionaire status all while maintaining a low profile, moving in the shadows of darkness.

Real was still working on his other two endeavors, the annihilation of All Things and Snake Eyes. He knew that trying to get at Snake Eyes and All Things at the same time would be a very unwise decision, so he devised a strategic master plan designed to defeat them both in due time. Real was eager to follow through with it, but told himself he was going to spend as much time with his baby mother and daughter as he could. This was just in case things didn't turn out right. For almost two months straight, Real and his family vacationed to different places and did any and everything that came to mind.

Real and Dynasty were inside their spacious living room of their new home with all the lights turned off. They were seated Indian style facing each other on the huge white bear rug a few feet away from the fire place drinking hot coco and feeding each other melted marshmallows. They just got out of the shower and were completely naked.

"Ah shit", Real said spitting out the marshmallow that burned his tongue.

Dynasty began chuckling while watching Real.

"Ain't nothing funny. You know damn well if something was to happen to my tongue and I was unable to use it ya ass would have a nervous break down", he said playfully.

Dynasty was a straight up sucker for Real's vicious tongue game and he knew it. Whenever he did something to make her angry, all he had to do was go down and lick it to make Dynasty forgive him.

"Umm hum. You right about that. I wouldn't be no more good", she responded seductively. "Matter fact, speaking of tongue..."

Dynasty crawled towards Real and gently grabbed his manhood, taking him into her wet mouth. Real let out a loud groan as he leaned back on his elbows, trying to keep his balance. He watched Dynasty's pink full lips and thick tongue go to work on his long rod. Dynasty stared deep into Real's lazy eyes as she sucked and twirled her tongue around the head of his throbbing penis.

During the wonderful time they spent together Dynasty was supposed to tell Real about how she pretended to be Snake Eyes wifey and learned everything there was to know about him. She was afraid of how he would react, so her words kept getting stuck in her throat when she started to tell him. Finally, after getting her courage up she told herself after she sucked the life out of Real and slammed her wet pussy on him she would bring everything to his attention. *After I give him some he's gonna be too at ease to flip*, she said to herself.

Dynasty grabbed Real's shaft and started jerking it while she sucked on his balls. She knew whenever she did this trick Real would bust a nut immediately, and feeling his body tense up she knew he was only a few seconds away. Dynasty looked up and noticed Real's eyes rolling behind his head. She then took the head of his penis and began sucking on it as if her life depended on it. Real threw his head back and let out an extremely loud grunt as he exploded in her mouth.

Dynasty was so turned on from Real's loud grunts and facial expression, juices from her warm honey pot dripped down her thick thighs onto the rug. After sucking the love of her life dry, she climbed on her hands and knees, turned around facing the fireplace, and bent all the way over face down ass up. She began shaking her voluptuous yellow ass, making it jiggle all over the place.

"Come get this wet pussy", she demanded seductively looking back at Real before licking her pink lips.

The sight of Dynasty's juicy booty jiggling caused Real's manhood to stiffen again, even harder than before. He knew exactly what she wanted, so he regained his composure and made his way over to his lady and began devouring her dripping wet love box from the back.

"Ahh Real", Dynasty moaned out loud as the sensation of Real's warm tongue licking on her swollen clitoris overpowered her.
Her loud moans turned him on. His strong hands sunk into Dynasty's soft ass cheeks as he grabbed hold to them and spread them out. He slid his wet tongue in between the crack of her ass slurping and eating greedily.

"Ahhh shit!" She continued to moan in ecstasy as she tightened her butt cheeks.

Dynasty wasn't used to getting her ass licked. The only time Real would bless her with this treatment was on special occasions. SLAP! Real smacked Dynasty on the ass, leaving his had print on her fanny. He then spread her soft but cheeks back out and began eating like a mad man. He worked his tongue fiercely from the crack of her anal to her soaking wet pussy, and then back to the crack of her ass, so on and so on, driving Dynasty wild.

Dynasty never felt anything so pleasant in her life. Real had his whole face buried in between her big ol' yellow ass. Face down ass up, Dynasty reached her hand down in between her thighs and began rubbing her swollen clitoris. The loud sound of Real slurping and the incredible feeling of his tongue was just too much to bear. Dynasty started having back to back orgasms, causing her whole entire body to tremble. "Ahhhhhhhh!" She roared as she squirted all over Real's face.

The intensity of the orgasm snatched her breath away. "Damn", she gasped in a low tone.

She struggled to catch her breath before turning to look back at Real who was on his knees. He took and held on to one side of her ass as he slid his rock hard manhood inside of her warm wetness. A low moan escaped Dynasty's lips as his thickness stretched her insides.

Real's strong hands gently grabbed hold to both of her luscious ass cheeks and spread them out as much as he could. He began digging deep inside of her with long, slow, but powerful strokes.

"Oooh I feel it in my stomach!" She moaned as she tightly grabbed hold to the fur rug.

Real looked down at Dynasty's creamy juices overflowing on his shaft as he passionately stroked in and out of her and immediately got more aroused than he already was.

"You feel it in ya stomach huh. Where you feel it at now?"

Real began stroking left, then right, then left and around and around in rotation. With is powerful strokes, Real dug as deep as he could possibly go inside of her wetness, hitting spots she never knew existed "Oh my...what are...what are you doing to me? What are you doing?" Dynasty moaned as she squirmed while staring at the red and blue fire flames.

Tears began to blur her vision. SLAP!
"What I tell you about running", Real said in between grunts.

Dynasty let out a low scream, turning back to look at Real. She immediately became overly excited at the sight of his chiseled chest and stomach muscles as he continued to stroke her deeply.

"Ummm. Stop playing and fuck this pussy good", she demanded as she sat up on all fours and began throwing her ass back wildly.

Without saying a word, Real quickly grabbed her by her long red hair and began beating it up relentlessly. Dynasty bit down on her bottom lip as her voluptuous titties and ass jiggled all over the place. She made sure to meet her man half way with every stroke. The sound of Real's balls smacking against

Dynasty's fat pussy lips was all you could hear throughout the living room.

Dynasty felt herself about to explode, so she lifted one of her legs up in the air, allowing Real to dig deeper into her honey pot. Her toes began to curl as she held on as tight as she could to the rug.

"Real! I'm cumming!"

Dynasty erupted all over Real's long pole. Within seconds Real came along with her, spitting his semen inside of her. Breathing heavily and covered in sweat he slid out of her and laid down on his back.

"Damn", he said before he reached his hand out to grab the pillow beside him, placing it under his head. "You alright baby?" Dynasty asked in an innocent tone.

She crawled over to him and laid beside him, resting her head on his chest. They were now cuddled up staring in to the fireplace.
"Yeah I'm good babes. I just feel a little drained", he responded while running his fingers through her long red hair.

"Yeah that's what a mean shot of this wet we will do to you", she said playfully.

Dynasty began rubbing on Real's rock hard abs. A lazy smile appeared on Real's face. "Yeah that's probably what did it. But I'm also drained mentally." He paused for a few seconds then continued. "I've been planning and plotting for almost two years how to get back at this snake ass nigga in the worst way. Now the time is finally almost here."

Real swallowed hard as he remembered how All Things murdered his father. He decided to keep that to himself for now, he would bring it to Dynasty's attention when he felt the time was right.

Dynasty could hear the mixed emotions in her man's voice, she could also feel his heart rate increase. She knew her baby dad hated Snake Eyes with a passion, and for that reason alone she too despised him just as much. *Should I tell him now?* She asked herself. *Fuck it.* "Baby it ain't no need to stress or bust ya' brain. It's gonna be way easier than you think to get back at that nigga, trust me", Dynasty assured.

Reals raised his eyebrows.
"Yeah I hope so, but what makes you so sure of it?" He asked.

Real always asked Dynasty if she saw Snake Eyes whenever she came back from Trenton, but she always told him no. An awkward silence filled the room for a few seconds, before Dynasty sat up and turned to look at Real in the face.

"Because...While I was in Trenton I pretended to be Snake Eyes' wifey and I learned everything there is to know about him and his organization so it would be easier for you to kill him and get all the money back he stole from you."

Real couldn't believe what he just heard and was flabbergasted. He didn't know whether to be mad at Dynasty for being up under his worst enemy and putting her life in danger, or be proud of her for being the down ass bitch that she was and making his job a whole lot easier.

Real stared at Dynasty for a few seconds as he analyzed the new information. Then he finally began talking.
"So you mean to tell me ya ass been lying to me all this time!"

"Baby I had to", Dynasty pleaded. "I knew if I would have told you what was going on before I found out everything you would've made me stop what I was doing. Please baby, I'm sorry. I was just trying to make things easier for you. I never had to sleep with him or none of that. He's infatuated with me, and will do whatever I tell him", she explained.

Although Real was extremely angry with his baby mother for lying to him and taking such a huge risk, he knew he had to over look it for the time being and take full advantage of the opportunity that was just brought to his attention. Real smirked and shook his head. "You crazy", he said, admiring his baby mother's bold cleverness.During the remainder of the night, Real and his ride or die baby mother stayed up devising a plan on how they were going to seek revenge on one of the most slimiest creatures that ever walked the earth, Snake Eyes.

CHAPTER 17

Real sent Dynasty to Trenton on a train to put their plan in motion. A few days before that he snatched up Wild Sal, J.J., and ten of his most deadliest henchmen. They packed up the heavy artillery and made their way to the small corrupted city of Trenton. They were ready for whatever!

It was early in the evening and Dynasty talked Snakes Eyes into spending majority of the day with her so Real and his crew would have more than enough time to seize all of the drugs and money from his stash houses scattered all over the county. First, they went to the mall and shopped all morning, then they made their way to an expensive soul food restaurant off of Route 1.

Dynasty and Snake Eyes sat across from one another in the crowded restaurant at a back table eating their food. Smooth jazz played to set the ambiance and mood.

"Next time you go down sssouth to visssit ya mom I'm coming", Snake Eyes said.

He was kind of upset at Dynasty for not answering her cell phone majority of the times he called her when she was down south.

"Damn baby alright. I was bringing you down there next time I went anyway", Dynasty replied in a soft tone.
"Oh you was huh."

"Yup, my mom said she want to meet you."

Dynasty took a spoon full of sweet corn as she glanced at the people sitting at the table a few feet away. Snake Eyes' eyes grew wide. Dynasty noticed the surprised look on his face and started laughing. *Yeah nigga, I'm gon' take ya ass to go talk to my mom alright*, she thought to herself deviously.

"Why you look like that", she asked.

Snake Eyes was so in shock that he didn't even hear what she just said.
"You wasss really talking to ya mom about me?"

"Yeah boy, don't get scared now", she responded with a smirk.

"SSSo what wasss y'all talking about?"
"Now you asking for too much information. What was talked about is between me and my mother. Now hurry up and eat so we can get up out of here and head back home."

Snake Eyes picked up his spoon and began slowly picking in it as if it was the worst meal he ate in his life. He had a loss of appetite, which was one of the may symptoms associated with the deadly virus he carried.

It was about 15 minutes and the two were pretty much done with their food.
"Damn, that was one of the best meals I had in a long time", Dynasty said yarning and stretching her hands in the air feeling full as a house.

"Yeah I know, we gotta ssstart coming to thisss ssspot more often."

Suddenly his stomach began bubbling and his bowels felt really loose as if he was bout to shit on himself. "Let me go use the bathroom Real quick before we leave", he said urgently.

Snake Eyes darted to the restroom holding his stomach. Once Dynasty saw him disappear into the back, she took out her cell phone and texted Real. WE SHOULD BE THERE IN 30 - 45 MINUTES. BE READY. She hurried to stuff her cell phone back into her purse. Several minutes later Snake Eyes came slowly walking from the restroom area.

"You ready?" He asked sounding exhausted as he approached Dynasty.
"Yeah I'm ready, but damn what took you so long?"

Snake Eyes began scratching his head. "That food fucked my stomach up."

Dynasty started walking towards the door, while Snake Eyes pulled out a wad of cash and placed the money for the bill on the table.

Meanwhile, Real sat in an all black Pacifica with dark tents in the enormous suburban apartment complex across the street from one of Snake Eyes' stash houses. The angle he was in made it hard for Dynasty and Snake Eyes to see him, but it also made it difficult for Real to

see them. That's why he had Wild Sal and J.J, along with several other henchmen, park their blue van on the other side of the housing complex so they could give him the signal when Snake Eyes pulled up.

Being that this was a very personal issue, Real wanted to come alone to put in work but Sal insisted he bring some back up just to be on the safe side.

Several minutes later Real felt his cell phone vibrating. "That must be my queue", he said to himself.

Real looked at the text message. THEY JUST PULLED INSIDE.
"It's on!", Real growled.

He grabbed his blue steel Beretta from off the passenger seat and cocked it back. CLICK! CLACK! Real tucked it in his front hoodie pocket, then quietly climbed out of his car and began creeping on the side of the big blue and white house.

Real heard two car doors shut before hearing his baby mother's loud laugh dance through the air. This was the signal letting him know it was go time. When he peaked his head out from the side of the house and saw Snake Eyes walk to the back of the car and pop the trunk, his blood began to boil and his heart burned with rage. A flood of emotions traveled through his body. The sight of Snake Eyes literally turned Real into a madman.

Dynasty stood several feet away from the car with shopping bags in both hands. Real noticed a couple of little girls a few feet away near the curb playing double dutch. *Damn it's little kids out here*, Real said to himself. He didn't want their innocent eyes to witness what was about to happen.

"Fuck it. This shit gonna be real quick and real slick."

Real eagerly made his way across the parking lot to Snake Eyes. After planning and plotting for almost 2 years, Real couldn't let this opportunity pass by. Snake Eyes grabbed the few bags out of the trunk and closed it. All of a sudden his heart dropped and his eyes grew wide as if they were going to pop out of his

head. Seeing the man he thought was dead and gone creeping up from behind through the reflection of the back window of his car stopped him dead in his tracks.

"Oh ssshit!"

Snake Eyes immediately dropped the bags and pulled out a black Uzi from his trunk and began shooting recklessly. *This bitch was setting me up the whole time*, he thought.

Real began squeezing at the same time. BLOW! BLOW! BLOW! BLOW! RAT! TAT! TAT! TAT! TAT! TAT! BLOW!

BLOW! BLOW! RAT! TAT! TAT! TAT! The rapid fire from Snake Eyes' Uzi was too much for Real's Beretta. He was able to back Real down ,sending him running sideways through the huge parking lot in search for a spot to duck for cover.

Out of nowhere a blue Taurus came speeding through the parking lot heading straight towards Real. Caught by surprise, he immediately dove out of the way onto the ground. It was Low Down coming to Snake Eyes' rescue once again, along with two other men from his squad. While Snake Eyes was in the bathroom at the soul food restaurant taking a shit, he called Low Down and told him to meet him at the money house so he could give him the bread he needed to meet up with the connect and re-up.

Dynasty quickly made her way behind a thick tall tree near the house and began shooting at the Taurus. Low Down slammed on the breaks causing the tires to screech. As he and the two other men got out of the car, Wild Sal sped inside the parking lot right in front of Real, blocking the storm of bullets that threatened to pierce him.

Wild Sal, J.J., and his crew quickly climbed out the van and joined the vicious gun battle. Real poked his head out from behind the van and surveyed the area for Snake Eyes, until he finally spotted him in the cut between two buildings.

"Where the fuck you think you going", he said to himself.

Real rushed towards him with his gun drawn. He was so determined to get at Snake Eyes that he paid no attention to the bullets that wizzed past his head and body. He was finally close enough to hit his prey. BLOW! BLOW! Real let off two shots hoping it would send Snake Eyes falling to the ground so he could get a chance to stand over top of him, stare into his eyes, and say a final farewell before killing him.

"Aghh!" Snake Eyes groaned in agony as the two hot slugs pierced through his upper back.

He stumbled forward, and it looked as if he was about to fall but he was able to catch his balance. He noticed one of the little girls that was playing double dutch crying while running beside him.

"Come here", he growled harshly, snatching the little girl up.

Snake Eyes put the machine gun to her head and quickly turned around to face Real. The little girl began screaming hysterically trying to brake loose from the monster's grasp.

"Help! Help! Daddy help me! Where are you daddy!" She cried.
"Damn!" Real barked in frustration.

He immediately stopped in his tracks with his gun still pointed at Snake Eyes. Real wanted so badly to just squeeze the trigger, but the sight and sound of the little girl's loud cries made him stop and think of his own daughter. *I can't shoot while this coward using this little girl as a shield*, Real said to himself.

A devilish grin crept across Snake Eyes' face. He knew Real wasn't going to bust his gun and jeopardize the life of an innocent child.
"If you try to follow me I'm gonna kill her!" Snake Eyes warned.

He still felt the extreme pain from the gunshot wounds in his back, so he quickly back peddled from in between the two houses and ran as fast as he could towards his car.

Real felt like a complete fuck up and fell down to his knees. He couldn't believe after having the perfect and probably the only opportunity to get back at the king cobra that bit him and the two people he loved dearly, he let him slip right out of his hands.
"What the fuck!", he roared.

Suddenly, the sound of Snake Eyes' machine gun woke him out of his remorseful trance. Before Snake Eyes pulled out of the apartment complex he murdered the little girl in cold blood. He wanted Real to know that he didn't save her life by not shooting him, and should've just handled his handle when he had the chance.

After hearing the shots, Real looked down sadly knowing exactly what just took place. He felt a burning sensation shoot through his leg, and looked down and noticed a huge blood stain in his jeans. Real was so caught up in the moment that he didn't feel when one of the bullets from the wild shootout pierced his leg when chasing behind Snake Eyes.

During the gun battle Low Down managed to get away with only one gunshot wound to the arm, but the other two men he came with didn't make it. Wild Sal rushed Real to the nearest hospital in the area where he got his gunshot wound treated. During the process the Feds and a few detectives blitzed the hospital, taking Real into their custody.

Coming in April!

New Books Coming Soon:

Cold World 3
Diamond in the Dirt 4 and 5
Color Blind
Teflon Divas
Scarlow: Return of the Black Don
Venom in My Veins: The Untold Story of Snake Eyes

Books Available Now:

Cold World 1 & 2

Diamond in the Dirt 1 & 2!